The Intrepid Women Series

Touch
Me

KATHRYN JANE

Acknowledgements

Many thanks to: my fabulous copy editor and formatter, Judi Fennell of www.formatting4U.com my brilliant cover artist, Jen Talty of Cool Gus Publishing; Brenda Novak for wonderful auction prizes; my amazing support team, Al, Barb and Judy; and my constant companions, providing warmth and comic relief, Wolfe and Bear.

Dedicated to
Bob, Nora, and Inish Glora...
you taught me to reach for my dreams, and to
celebrate.

Table of Contents

Chapter 1	01
Chapter 2	17
Chapter 3	30
Chapter 4	40
Chapter 5	49
Chapter 6	55
Chapter 7	65
Chapter 8	72
Chapter 9	83
Chapter 10	93
Chapter 11	101
Chapter 12	111
Chapter 13	117
Chapter 14	127
Chapter 15	133
Chapter 16	143
Chapter 17	152
Chapter 18	161
Chapter 19	170
Chapter 20	180
Chapter 21	192
Chapter 22	201
Chapter 23	211
Chapter 24	218
Chapter 25	226
Chapter 26	233
Chapter 27	240
Chapter 28	247
Chapter 29	255
Dear Reader	263
Excerpt from Book 1 - Do Not Tell Me No	265
Excerpt from Book 3 - Daring to Love	271
Author Bio	276

Chapter 1

Grace shuddered as unbearable memories fought to surface.

She wrenched open the door and stepped into a whirling of unfamiliar energy.

Heart slamming against her ribs, she scanned the garage, saw the smooth concrete and shiny cars one would expect. She tipped her head, opened her senses, and listened carefully.

Nothing. Just nerves, she thought. Must beat the panic. Stay in control. Get to the car.

But the parking spot was empty—except for the sign on the wall she'd missed when she'd arrived. With a groan at her own stupidity, she scurried back to the elevator room and grabbed the doorknob. It refused to open. She circled to the other door, but it, too, was locked.

Frustration took the edge off her fear.

"Five floors below the flippin' city and I have to walk out," she muttered as she began the trek. Narrow spiked-heels assaulted the concrete with angry intent, echoes bounced, while a new tingling of awareness crawled up her spine.

Logan held his position at the side window of the surveillance vehicle, adrenaline hovering, waiting at the edge. A warning flickered through him before he heard the sound. He slipped his hand into the black curtain, edged it open a fraction, and, for a moment, he was just a man, not a special agent.

The woman was stunning. Long, lean, sun-kissed skin with dark silk sliding over sexy curves.

"Son of a bitch." he growled.

"What? What is it?" The team leader's voice rattled through his earpiece.

"I thought they secured this place."

"Done. Elevator doors electronically frozen. Garage doors same."

"Bullshit. There's a woman walking toward me."

"What?"

She was less than fifty feet away now. He sucked in a breath and muttered, "Drop-dead-fucking-gorgeous-woman."

Her head came up like a startled gazelle.

Carter's voice cut in. "Shit. Get her contained. We can't have a civilian in the middle of this. Into the van now! Two minutes max to target."

Logan slipped out and watched her from behind a concrete pillar.

She stopped, eyes wide, searching, took a couple more steps then leaned down to jerk off her shoes. The slit up the side of her skirt gaped open. He tore his attention away from the long smooth leg in time to catch a glimpse of luscious breast pressing against the top of the silky dress. She straightened, reached up to push the sun streaked mass of hair back from her face, and he stepped in front of her, badge in hand.

"Police, ma'am."

He barely saw the flash of panic in her golden eyes before she spun and ran for her life.

"Shit." Caught flat-footed, he dug deep to catch up.

"What?" Carter's voice came through the earpiece. "What's going on?"

"Rabbit," he growled as he stretched to grab her by the shoulder.

"*NO!*" she screamed, twisting around with every ounce of flight morphing into fight and driving her knee deep into his groin.

"*Ugh.*" It was a grunt, followed by a groan and other unintelligible guttural sounds, pieces of words. Hot seething pain shot up through him, sucked the breath from his lungs. Her arm swung and he took the full force of shoes—with matching evening bag—across his left ear. There was a gasping, scuffling noise and a couple more grunts.

Earpieces suddenly crackled with, "Man down! Paul, Lance, level three!"

She kicked, punched, scratched, and clawed but he didn't let go, kept up the battle, unsure if he was trying to save her life or his own. There'd been one clear moment when he could have tagged her, dropped her, knocked the fight right out of the bitch. Instead, still half bent, gasping for breath while nausea clawed at him, he snagged her wrists, held them behind her back, and ground out, "Police, dammit. Knock it off."

Only then did he hear them. First the hard boots pounding, then, "Police!" and she was ripped away from him to be held firmly between two heavily armored S.W.A.T. officers. Bent double now, his forearms pressing on his thighs, he tipped his head and saw the confusion on her face. *Realization at war with the need to be free and probably the bloody gender's need to be right.*

Carter's voice was sharp and urgent in his earpiece. "Target on approach. Positions. Move!"

The two black-clad figures shoved her back at him and vanished among the parked cars.

There was no time. They were too far away from the van. Never make it. He could already hear the vehicle, tires squealing gently on the tight turns between levels. His voice was low and deadly serious as he tugged her back between cars. "This is life or death, lady, so play along." He dragged her against him, pulled her arms up around his neck, wrapped his own around her waist, and growled, "Pretend you're liking it." Then his mouth dropped over hers.

His senses were swamped, his brain on overdrive trying to concentrate on headlights, path, speed, and her knee settling firmly between his with unmistakable intent. Voices in his earpiece. Excruciating pain, and the taste of his own blood. He didn't flinch, didn't try to save himself, but kept his eyes on the taillights while holding her firmly in place.

Finally, Carter gave him the word. "Logan, clear."

His hand slid up, wrapped around her throat and squeezed until her teeth released his bottom lip.

She opened her mouth to speak, but he tightened his hand on her throat, stared into angry eyes that made him think of jungle cats, and listened intently to Carter's voice in his ear.

"Shit," he muttered and she watched him begin to

scan the area. His hands slid to her arms tightening, forcing her toward the ground, then pushing, shoving her under a bright red car. He left her there, moved away, vanished.

Grace held her breath while she listened for a moment, heard nothing, then wormed her way further under until she felt completely hidden from view. Her senses struggled for information. The concrete against her back was smooth, cold. Above her there was some kind of black stuff on the underside. Of course, undercoat. She'd had that done to her car too, didn't know why for sure, just part of some package deal.

There was that tingling sensation again.

Then, suddenly, all hell broke loose. Shouting. Pounding feet. Screeching tires. Gunfire. The smell settled like rancid oil in the back of her throat. She pressed her hands over her ears, squeezed her eyes shut, and willed herself not to shriek in mindless terror. There was no voice in her head now, no coaching, no instruction, no argument. She'd been programmed for survival and that was what took over. She lay perfectly still, barely breathing.

Eventually, she began to think, to notice the silence. A fist clamped hard on her heart when her mind registered the faint but unmistakable sharp-edged smell of gunfire. And blood. Tears slipped from her eyes. Her hands moved from her ears to her mouth, ready to smother any sound attempting to escape. And she waited for the pain, the horrors likely to follow.

She tried to distract herself with thoughts of Milo, how happy he'd be to see her. He hated when she left him for too long. She'd make it up to him, let him spend the night in her bed.

#

Parking Level Five was awash with people. Men in black armor moved about, restless, oozing adrenaline, still. The perp, the target, the reward, lay dead on the concrete. There would be no day in court, no final opportunity for victims to tell him how it felt to lose loved ones, no watching him dragged off to the electric chair. No closure. The bastard was dead. Took the coward's way out, suicide by cop, cheated everyone... One last time.

Logan drew a deep breath as the Medical Examiner's car came to a stop, its grill just touching the yellow tape strung across the open space. This was it. This was when he had to let go and walk away, hand over control to the local authorities, case closed, let the paperwork begin.

A second car pulled up, parked behind the ME's wagon and Nancy Tomkins hefted herself out of the driver's seat. Skin the color of molasses, hair pulled back and held securely in some kind of knot, and wearing a plain denim dress, she could be anyone. Until she smiled. And then the warm just leaked out everywhere.

She could pick people up, dust 'em off, and walk them through the system with the kind of ease that made it look like a stroll in the park on a Sunday afternoon.

Carter spoke to her for a minute before he motioned Logan over. "Hey, where did you leave that woman? Victim's Assistance is here to debrief her."

"Shit." Logan ran a hand over his face. "Under a red Beemer, a couple of levels up."

"Jesus, Logan."

He scowled. "Hey we were kinda busy here, dammit." He turned and started to walk.

Nancy kept pace beside him. She understood the scenario. Cops getting caught up in the situation didn't notice the eyes around them, let alone the souls. Forgetting about victims until the adrenaline wore off, then feeling like shit. His hand rubbed at the back of his neck.

"How is this woman involved, Logan?"

"Somehow slipped through the perimeter. Innocent bystander. Perp was coming in, I had to stop her. Get her out of the way. She freaked, I shoved her under a car to keep her out of the line of fire."

He stepped between a black Escalade and a red BMW.

"Safe to come out now." He crouched and reached for her. "Give me your hands."

Long fingers gripped Logan's. He saw a fine line, a scar running palm to elbow on the inside of her left arm. Then he heard the whisper of a voice in his mind, *Mother of God, how can this be fair?*

Grace, once clear of the car, sat up, her head swimming. Barely able to register his hands under her armpits lifting her to her feet, she failed to object to his fingertips brushing the sides of her breasts as he straightened her dress. Her gaze was locked on that of the woman standing behind him. She blinked and came out of her shocked stupor to breathe a single word. "Nancy."

"Oh, honey how could this be happening to you?" Nancy opened her arms and Grace, in a single move that would have stunned most who knew her, stepped into them.

"Are you okay, honey? Hurt anywhere? Where are your shoes, girl?"

Grace smiled, savoring the warmth of this mother-of-all. "God, I'm glad to see you."

Nancy stroked her hand over the tangled brown and gold hair and teased, "Honey, how'd you get yourself wedged under that itty bitty car? Why didn't you pick yourself a bigger spot to hide?"

"Didn't have a choice. Brontosaurus here just grabbed and shoved. Not much for manners."

Nancy looked over at Logan. "What'd you do to my girl?"

Obviously outnumbered and instantly on the defensive, he said, "Just tried to save her friggin' life, Nan. No thanks necessary."

Grace straightened away from Nancy and snarled, "You took advantage of the situation, whatever the hell it was, and had the gall to kiss me. You had no right."

"Hell, woman, you'd already crammed my nuts up around my ears. Figured I might as well go for broke."

Nancy bit back a snicker. "She—?"

He nodded.

"And you kissed her *after* that?"

"The perp was driving past us. Had to shut her up somehow and hide my face at the same time. Who gives much notice to a couple making-out in the parking garage, you know? Seemed like the right thing to do at the time."

"I can certainly see your point. I'm sure he didn't mean any harm by it, Grace. It was a smart tactical move."

"Huh. Well he won't be quick to try those *tactics* again anytime soon."

"Damn sure." He touched his throbbing lip. "Probably need stitches. Hope you've had a recent rabies shot." He looked at Nancy. "Am I done here?"

"Yeah. I'll take care of Grace. You go finish up. I'll get your paperwork tomorrow."

Logan started to walk away, but couldn't resist. He took one last look over his shoulder and thought, *yup, even all messed up and scowling, the bitch was still gorgeous.* He shook his head. B*ut lethal. No doubt about that either.*

#

Buried amid a vast array of cold, impersonal conference rooms on the third floor of police headquarters, Nancy's office was a warm, cozy, safe haven.

Lush potted plants filled shelves, hung from ceiling hooks, and perched on wide windowsills. Walls painted old-denim blue created a soft background to mismatched furniture in shades of brown, from taffy to dark chocolate. A scattering of rainbow-bright cushions drew the eye like candy. Nancy's desk, unobtrusive in the corner, was smooth and curved.

Grace tossed back four aspirin and tucked herself into a corner of the leather couch. With a sky blue pillow in her lap and her legs curled under her, she cupped a heavy tiger-lily-orange mug between her hands, stared out the window into the darkness and tried not to listen to Nancy's phone conversation.

Nancy hung up and smiled at her. "Your car's

been found."

"Where?"

The smile was wry. "Exactly where you left it."

She frowned. "But it wasn't there."

"Honey, you must have taken the wrong elevator and ended up in the other parking garage. The hotel has two. One for residential monthly parking and the other for daily use."

Grace closed her eyes. "And I'm not even blonde."

Nancy threw back her head and laughed. "Never mind, honey. Even us black girls have our moments. Anyhow, Logan will bring it here for you when he's done."

"Brontosaurus jerk," she muttered.

"Hey, he's not so bad. Kept you safe, didn't he?"

Grace ignored that. "He was still pissy even after the shooting was over. Got his man, didn't he? Should've been happy about it."

"Perp's dead."

"Even better. Perfect ending for a bad guy, don't you think?"

Nancy smiled ruefully. "No retribution that way. No justice served."

"Yeah, no court cases, technicalities, high-paid lawyers, screaming families, media feeding frenzies... Like I said, perfect fucking ending."

Time to change the subject. "How about we get your statement now so you'll be free to go when he gets here?"

"What statement?"

"Come on, Grace. Victim's Assistance protocol, you know the drill. Statement now, then go home and get some sleep. I'll check in with you again tomorrow to make sure you're okay. See if you want to add anything."

"But I'm not a victim. I wasn't involved, didn't see anything, anyone, don't know what happened. And don't care."

"Easy, honey. I understand you were an innocent bystander. Wrong place, wrong time. But I still need your statement in order to protect Logan, just in case you decide a year from now to sue for police brutality."

"Oh, for crying out loud, you know I wouldn't do that."

"I know, but I have to follow procedure. You got roughed up by… one of our boys, I need the story in writing. Why don't you start with why you were in that parking garage tonight?"

Grace sighed. "My mother was throwing one of her infamous launch parties. You know, a couple hundred of her closest friends gathered together for fancy food and free champagne. In exchange, they stroke her ego while she sings several songs from her new album. But of course, to warm them up, she opens with a couple of her old hits."

Nancy sat quietly, waiting for Grace to continue.

"I'm sure you've already guessed. She sang *Born to Dance.*" Grace took a long, deep breath. "She knows what that song does to me, the memories it triggers, the panic attacks that follow. But she stared right at me and smiled. Said this was her darling daughter's song."

Grace grimaced, tipped her head back against the couch, closed her eyes and let the memory take hold.

#

The ice-cold, blue-eyed challenge had been warning enough. Grace didn't need to hear the cotton candy words that followed.

"*Born to Dance* is a song I wrote many years ago for my darling daughter who has *graced* us with her presence tonight." Meredith's tiny, perfect, well-maintained body swayed with the opening notes.

Grace's eyes narrowed, unflinching as anger boiled up inside her. Jaw clenched, her chin came up ever so slightly. She'd stand there if it killed her. Meredith had thrown out the challenge, virtually saying, 'Grow up, Grace. Get over yourself'. And by God she'd stand.

Back teeth grinding against each other, fingernails digging into her palms, and backbone stiff, she fought the demons.

And as always, failed. The music swept through her, left her unsettled, confined, needing air. Then everything escalated. A great weight pressed on her soul, her lungs strained, her heart banged frantically against her ribs. Her fingertips tingled. She was suffocating. Even her skin screamed for air. Colors and lights bled into each other, blending and sparkling—too bright.

She had to get out of here.

Running, from the back exit to a service elevator, ridiculously sure-footed on four inch heels, she didn't even think to be surprised when the door slid open as she reached it. She dove in, pounded her fist against the 'door close' button, gasped for air, and as the elevator descended and the music faded above her, she slumped against the quilt-covered wall, moaning.

The sound, the vibration in her own throat penetrated the haze of panic. She drew a deep breath and held it. The expected pain in her head was already starting and the evening bag she clutched held nothing to help her. Fingers shook and stalled over the operational panel. She couldn't face the underground parking. Not yet. Nor could she deal with all the eyes in the lobby. Not like this.

She punched the button marked Pool, it would have to do.

Stepping from the musty-smelling elevator into a maze of luxurious potted palms, she was enveloped by moist chlorine-scented air as she followed discrete little brass signs to the deserted patio.

Fighting tiny flashes of light inside her head, she worked at slowing her breathing and rationalizing. It didn't matter that she'd left, only three songs into Meredith's performance. She'd already done her daughterly duty, put in an appearance, nodded and smiled sweetly, laughed softly on cue. Done as her mother expected, received the same back, and more. She'd met those big blue eyes and seen the dare, been determined to win but still the panic had come.

She felt the sweat on her skin as it cooled. Her heart rate returned to normal and pure aggravation settled like an itch between her shoulder blades. She crouched to slide her fingers through the warm softness of the water. Long slow laps would work wonders to ease her nerves, stall the inevitable headache. She sighed. *First get home, then have your swim and a nice cold beer before falling into bed.*

Grace found a ladies' room, and smiled faintly as

she pushed open the door. She could at least have comfort for the drive home. She stripped off her panties and the claustrophobic stockings, dropping them into a garbage bin. Then she unfastened the strapless bra, pulled it out the front of her dress, and stuffed it into her evening bag. From thin jeweled straps, the coffee-colored silk now hung soft and cool against her naked skin.

She grinned at her reflection in the mirror. "Why, you loose woman, you." Then she muttered. "And not a man in sight. Pity." She plucked the solid gold pick from her elegantly knotted hair and shook it free to fall soft and thick as a lion's mane around her shoulders.

She marched through the doorway and down the hall with purpose in her step. But her confidence evaporated when the elevator door opened and a tall gray-haired man in a dark suit stood before her.

"Down?" he asked quietly.

"No," she stammered, abruptly spun away to stride back toward the pool. *Stupid. Afraid to get into an elevator with a poor innocent stranger. Somebody's grandfather, for heaven's sake. Yet here I am, all alone by the pool instead?* She wandered among the palm and banana trees until she calmed down, then again found the elevator, this time descending to Parking Level Four.

She stepped out, tentative, listening, gaze darting around the tiny hollow space, and headed toward a heavy metal door. Those were the worst: doors that opened into the unknown.

She sucked a breath in through her teeth and carefully exhaled out her nose. She wished she could close her eyes for just a second but didn't dare. The metal knob felt cool against her sweaty palm. *Grip, turn, push.*

Thick stale air swept in, swirled around her, invaded her lungs. Her heart slammed against her ribs. She ran back and hammered the heel of her hand against the elevator's Up *and* Down buttons, while the pounding of her own heart tried to swallow her up.

Nancy cleared her throat. "Grace?"

Grace opened her eyes and blinked a couple of times. "Sorry."

"Can you tell me what happened?"

"The usual. The song sent me into a panic attack and I bolted. I stopped at the pool level to calm down. I was feeling claustrophobic by then and–" She managed a twisted little smile. "I hit the ladies' room, stripped off the stockings and bra, and let my hair down. When I headed to my car, it wasn't where I'd left it. The doors to the elevator room locked behind me so I started to walk out, pissed by then instead of panicky. That's when I ran smack into the Brontosaurus. He shoved his badge in my face and growled, 'Police.'"

"That's when you nailed him?"

She grimaced. "Nope, first I ran for my life. But he caught me. So that's when I kneed his nuts north of the equator."

#

Half an hour passed and most of the forms had been filled out before they were interrupted by a loud knock on the door. When Nancy opened it, Logan stepped into the room and placed a huge manila envelope on her desk.

"Victim's property. Car's parked out front." He smirked at Grace, grinned at Nancy, then backed out and closed the door with a *click*.

Nancy was smiling. "Well, he seems to have recovered his pleasant demeanor." She handed the envelope to Grace who dumped the contents onto the table in front of her and grimaced.

"Touché asshole."

"Now what?"

Grace held up the sexy, coffee-brown, strapless bra that matched the dress she was wearing. "A nice guy would have stuffed it back into the handbag and left me to think he hadn't seen it."

Nancy grinned. "Game, point, and match."

Grace laughed, unable to help herself.

After another hour of friendly conversation and a promise from Grace that she'd share tonight's event with her grief counselor, Nancy walked her to the navy blue Mercedes parked at the curb.

#

From his window, Logan watched them. "Nancy the anchor" had held another one together. The nasty beauty was smiling when she left.

Chapter 2

Downright drained by the panic attack and her terrifying experience in the parking garage, Grace let her guard down. She failed to check call display before answering the phone when she arrived home. Now she was stuck in a conversation she'd hoped not to have. She rolled her shoulders. "Mother, it was not a big deal, for crying out loud."

"But the press, Grace. If they get wind of your involvement in *another* murder, it will cast a pall over my party and people will begin to think my daughter invites trouble. There will be headlines about you being a bad omen. What will people think? How will it affect the release of my new album?"

Why you insensitive bitch. Your precious image is all you've ever cared about.

"Mother, it won't be hitting the news at all. It's really a quiet deal. Top Secret, actually. The cops threw around words like *Classified*, so if it gets leaked to the press, it will be your fault, not mine." She crossed her fingers before she lied. "They said they'd press charges against anyone talking to the media."

"Well," her mother huffed. "It's not as if *I'd* do something like that."

Grace leaned her forehead against the wall. The woman would, in fact, do anything she could to get her name in the media.

"Mother, I just mean you'd best not trust anyone else with information about the incident in the garage because if *they* let anything slip, you'll be the one to pay. And you know, media attention is one thing, but the kind of people involved in what happened tonight shoot first and ask questions later."

"I understand what you're saying; I'm just offended you'd think one of my people would be so irresponsible."

"Please, Mother, I'm just the messenger. I'm repeating the warning for your own good—so you can keep yourself and your people safe." Grace pushed her fingertips against the escalating pain between her eyes and held the phone away from her ear while the voice went on and on. Why the hell did Meredith's manager have to go and blab about what he'd seen? Why hadn't he called her instead? Jerk.

Grace held the phone a few inches away from her mouth. "Mother, my battery is almost dead." She moved the phone even farther. "I'll call you tomorrow." Now she held it at arm's length. "Bye-bye, Mother. The party was lovely and you sounded fabulous as always."

Grace placed the phone in the charger even though it didn't need it, reached into the fridge for a beer, and hesitated. This headache would need some of the good stuff. She closed the door and went to the bathroom for prescription meds. Back in the kitchen, she popped several pills and chased them with chocolate milk. She didn't care what the doctors claimed about chocolate and headaches. If she couldn't have a beer to soothe her frazzled nerves, she'd damn well have the next best thing.

She stared out into the darkness and wondered if she should throw a sleeping pill on top of the rest. Better not. Bad enough to be using pain-killers this often. Instead, she went to the patio door, placed her palm against the security panel, waited for the green light, and slid the glass open.

Milo stepped out of his heated doghouse and stretched. She knelt to hug him and apologized for being out so late. She hated leaving him outside, but he was only happy indoors when she was at home. When they'd met, he was a skinny, muddy mess, slinking around the stables, sneaking bites from the barn cat's dish. Failing to find his owners, Grace had adopted him and learned plenty about what the scrawny black dog did and didn't like. He let out a series of whines now, his tailless black rump wriggling happily.

Jesus, she thought, it must be like trying to smile without lips. The expression had to take over his whole body. She shook her head. *Definitely time to shut off the mind.*

Standing at the edge of the pool, surrounded by the blackness and silence of night, she pushed the jeweled straps from her shoulders so the battered silk dress slid to the cool tiles. She lifted her arms over her head with the smooth elegance of a seasoned ballerina, rose up on her toes, pushed off, and arched her body, diving shallow and fast into the cool, dark water. Self-discipline kept her below the surface until she'd completed two full laps before coming up for air.

Milo's whining greeted her as she took the first breath and began making long, sweeping strokes. He shadowed her, trotting along the pool's edge while she settled into the motion, lap after lap, mindless, boneless, fluid like the water, one arm after the other, one breath every other stroke, long lazy turns. When the weight of anxiety lifted, leaving her free and in control, she continued pushing for another twenty laps, then ten more, seeking exhaustion, the kind that would allow her to sleep tonight.

Utterly spent when her feet finally touched bottom, she stood chest deep with a panting Milo hovering above her. She grinned. "Had enough, big boy?"

He lay down and hung his head over the edge for a drink. She splashed water at him. "Don't do that, you idiot. Go to your dish." Chlorinated pool water always disagreed with his belly and would come back up on the kitchen floor in mere minutes. She splashed again and he waited for her to climb up the ladder before heading for his water dish.

Grace glanced at the clock. Three hundred hours. She locked up, reset security, took a quick shower, and fell into bed, praying the combination of meds and exercise would keep the pain at bay.

#

At four in the morning Nancy walked down the hall and stuck her head into the conference room. "You still at it?"

Logan looked up. "Yeah. Fucking guy offs himself and I get stuck with the paperwork. He shoulda had to do all this before he stepped into the bullets."

"Sounds like you'd better get some sleep before you finish up." She nodded toward the files on the table in front of him. "Chances are you'll have to redo them when you regain some of your good humor in the morning anyhow."

"How's Ms. Espresso?"

"Who?"

"Dame with the attitude."

"Why'd you call her *espresso*?"

"Looks like damn good coffee but tastes bitter as hell."

"Ah, so nothing to do with the color of her underwear?"

"Bra. She wasn't wearing panties." The corners of his mouth twitched. "Or the bra for that matter."

"Why didn't you stuff it back in the purse?"

"My balls are black and blue, I have a hole in my bottom lip, a shoe imprint alongside my ear, and I'm supposed to be courteous? A little embarrassment was the least she deserved."

"She had no right to defend herself from an unknown assailant?"

His shoulders went back. "She squawked self-defense?" He shook his head. "I told her I was police. Showed her my badge. She rabbits, I catch her. Then wham, the leg I'd been admiring seconds earlier, turns lethal. Knocks the air clean out of me, *then* she goes berserk."

"Extenuating circumstances. She's really a lovely person."

"To look at from a safe distance maybe. One-way

glass would be even better."

Nancy laughed. "Not saying you should ever get any closer, just that there's a good reason for the beating you got."

"Sure there is. She hates men, right? Plays for the other team? Christ, it's always the good-looking ones." He shook his head.

"And you call yourself an investigative specialist."

His eyes narrowed. "What the hell does that mean?"

"Put your bruised ego on ice for a minute and think about tonight, hotshot."

He frowned at her. Hated being scolded. Ran it through from the beginning to the end when he delivered the envelope with her stuff. She'd been curled up on the sofa in Nancy's office. Looked comfortable, as if she belonged there. His mind flashed back to when he'd lifted her to her feet and she'd seen Nancy. Jesus, he'd let that go by, too pissed at her, pissed at himself for leaving her under the car for so long. Couldn't believe he'd flat-ass forgotten about her.

"Okay, she's not just a friend of yours. You know her as a victim."

"Very good."

He thought about the look on her face when he'd flashed his badge. "Shit. Don't tell me she was assaulted by a cop impersonator." He'd worked something similar in Florida.

"Not quite, but see if this rings any bells for you. Mugging in a downtown parking garage, man dies from a single gunshot wound, woman's sliced, nearly bleeds to death. Cold case, never solved."

"Sonofabitch." He closed his eyes. "I've read it. Perp flashes a badge, catches them off guard with the knife, gets a few hundred cash. Man goes for his gun, ankle piece, scuffling, man's gut-shot, woman's cut, perp gets away, lover dies in her arms."

He scrubbed at his face. "And that was her? How the hell did she end up in that garage tonight? Is there no such thing as pity among the gods?"

"Funny, she asked me the same thing."

"So what's the answer?"

"There isn't one." She pinned him with an unwavering gaze. "Maybe you just have to look at it from a different angle and wonder what the message is."

#

Grace endured the pain, tossing and turning until after seven, before she reached for the pill bottle in the nightstand. She talked herself out of a handful of the tiny pink pills, dumped two onto her palm, and washed them down with tepid water from the glass beside her bed.

Oblivion was hers until nine-thirty when the phone on the nightstand began an unrelenting buzz. She pulled the pillow over her head but Milo pawed it away. She gave in and picked up the receiver.

"House better be on fire," she growled.

"Nope."

She hung up, but the buzzing sounded again. Face still half-under the pillow, she grabbed the offending hunk of plastic. "Go. Away."

"Grace, let me in," said Nancy.

She heaved a sigh. "Let yourself in." She propped herself up on one elbow. "And plug in the kettle."

Logan wasn't surprised at the irritation so obvious in the woman's voice. "Still sounds pretty wicked to me."

"She'll be better when she wakes up. Must have taken something," Nancy muttered. "It's not like her to be in bed at this time of day." She stuck her hand into what looked like a mail slot at waist level. When a tiny green light appeared next to the lock, she used her key to open the door.

The security system's energy prickled around Logan's spine as he walked through the door, but it dissipated as they climbed two flights of stairs to the kitchen. The house was built against a hill with the entrance on the lowest floor and the backyard three floors up.

While Nancy went about setting up for tea, Logan studied the kitchen and adjoining room. The stark white furniture, cupboards, and walls would have been blinding but for the generous scattering of colorful items. Looked like all her dishes and things were lime green. She'd stuffed about a dozen containers the color of blue cotton candy with flowers, and all her mixers and whatnot were Popsicle orange.

Double pocket doors separating the kitchen from an informal office were three-quarters open. The windows behind the desk were securely latched, and he'd be willing to bet there was a safe behind an enormous painting of ocean waves.

His gaze moved to the no-nonsense lap pool outside. Long and narrow with no diving board. One ladder. Two wooden slatted lounge chairs were separated by a small matching table. A tidy gazebo to one side looked to be an outdoor office with a desk, chair, and cabinet.

He gave up trying to ignore the puddle of dark silk on the pale blue tiles—the dress she'd been wearing the night before—imagined her long elegant fingers pushing the thin rhinestone straps from her shoulders, her arms raising slowly, her hands reaching for the moonlight as dark silk melted downwards, exposing the smooth golden length of her. She'd arc in a graceful dive to have the cool water caress her flesh as she stroked the length of the pool. His skin grew warm.

A sudden flash of four-legged white fur, then black, raced through the room, and Grace, her tangled hair pushed behind her ears and wearing nothing but a faded brown terrycloth robe, followed on their heels. "Milo, leave the cat alone for heaven's sa—" The rest of her words went unsaid when she caught sight of him. She swung to Nancy. "Why didn't you tell me you weren't by yourself?"

"Would've, had you been listening." She grinned.

Without another word, Grace spun and left the room.

"Something tells me she's not gonna be quite as sweet as you thought today." Logan grimaced. "Maybe I should leave before I suffer more bodily harm."

"Don't you dare." Nancy's tone left no room for argument, right or wrong.

Suspecting a set-up, there was little he could do but stand there and take it. *So this would be payback.* With a mental shrug, he bent down and made friends with both Milo and the big white cat.

By the time Grace reappeared, Nancy had placed a teapot, cups, spoons, milk, and sugar on the table along with an opened box of doughnuts.

Logan took in Grace's changed appearance thinking she might as well have donned a protective shield. Black pants with a hard front crease, crisp white shirt complete with stand-up collar and sharp-edged cuffs under a black-and-gray plaid vest made her look like a store mannequin. She'd even put on black loafers and tamed her hair into a tight knot secured by a shiny black clip.

Looking at a total contradiction to the woman from the night before, he thought about the bra she'd had in her purse, the lack of stockings, even panties, as though she preferred comfort. Or was it speed—maybe she'd just left her lover's bed...

"Have you drawn any conclusions yet detective?" Brassy eyes stared him down.

"Pardon?" He blinked.

"You've been studying me for about three minutes. Care to wager what color underwear I'm wearing?"

He didn't miss a beat. "Black of course. You'll be coordinated right down to the skin."

She flashed a smile that didn't reach her eyes, undid the middle button of the vest, then the blouse, inserted her thumb and pulled a bit of shiny crimson satin into view. "Point's mine."

She did the buttons back up and said to Nancy, "So I know you have to do a follow-up to make sure I didn't fling myself off a building during the night, but why did you bring the Brontosaurus with you?"

Nancy chuckled. "Are you always this grumpy when you wake up?"

"Only when I've been frightened half to death, manhandled by a total stranger, drugged myself into oblivion, been woken up only two hours into the first sleep I've had since sometime yesterday morning, and find unexpected, judgmental company in my kitchen."

Nancy didn't flinch. "Trouble sleeping, honey? You should have taken something when you got home."

Grace rolled her eyes. "Shoulda... did. Got a cupboard full of colorful pills to choose from. Something small and pink a few hours ago finally worked, but here I am awake again and nothing I say can be held against me." Her temper faded with the last words.

Logan had been watching her. "Why don't you go back to bed? We can talk tomorrow." His voice was soft and low

Her jaw clenched. "What could we possibly have to talk about?"

Nancy jumped in. "Nothing much. Logan was just worried about you after last night, and we both had business over this way today so I thought you wouldn't mind a visit."

Grace's eyes narrowed. "It's not like you to lie to me, Nancy. You told him, didn't you?" She focused on Logan. "All right. So I've got a little 'traumatic history.' Don't sweat it, Brontosaurus. I'm no china doll. Been through hell, survived. No big deal." She pointed at the box on the table. "You brought doughnuts. Eat one for heaven's sake." Her gaze met his and locked on for more than a heartbeat while she gritted her teeth.

Her bright golden eyes had dulled, tarnished by exhaustion and pain.

Nancy broke the silence. "Grace, could we come back in a couple of hours? Maybe say, two-ish?"

"Why?"

"We have to go to a meeting right now, but there's something we need to talk to you about. Take a couple of hours. Sleep, relax, do something to bring back your sunny disposition."

Logan was still watching her eyes. "You get migraines?"

"Yeah, why?"

"You've got a doozy comin' on."

"Wrong again, Detective." She winced. "Migraine fully engaged."

He placed his hands on her shoulders, pointed her toward the door, and with the faintest of pushes said, "Go to bed. We'll be in touch tomorrow."

Grace started to nod, thought better of it, barely heard Nancy say, "I'll feed the animals and reset security before we leave. Call me if you need anything."

She shrugged, left them, didn't care if they stayed or not, suddenly desperate for darkness, silence, a soft place to die. She left a trail of clothing across her bedroom and crawled under the comforter, naked, face down. She heard a faint noise and cracked open one eye. The Brontosaurus was setting a fresh glass of water on her night table.

What a beautiful hand. Long, strong, fingers. Her wish was little more than a sigh. *Touch me.*

The soft words stroked Logan's mind. Silent and

wary, he waited. She didn't move so much as an eyelash, but he heard it again. *Touch me.* He sat on the edge of the bed, carefully eased the black clip from her hair, tunneled his fingers into the mass of sun-streaked brown hair, and gently massaged the tension in her scalp. His thumbs worked the taut muscles at the base of her skull until he could feel her slipping into unconsciousness.

Help me. Her voice was the barest whisper in his mind as her words tumbled quickly, made little sense, and then... silence.

His fingertips skimmed the back of her neck as he wondered, *why?*

Chapter 3

Leaving Grace's house, they drove for a while in silence before Nancy asked, "Ever considered working Victim's Unit?"

"No."

"You should. That was a good read on her, Logan."

He gave Nancy a sharp look. "What does that mean?" Had she heard the voice, too?

"The headache. Ashamed to say I'd missed it altogether. Just thought she was being cranky because I'd brought you along."

"Been around a migraine or two myself, that's all. Just happen to know they look more like plain old crabbiness sometimes." His ex had driven him nearly senseless in the name of "migraine" more than a few times before they'd finally parted. He knew the look. Knew how to handle it. And even before he'd heard the voice, he'd known there was something different about this woman's headache. He just couldn't put his finger on what the difference was. Yet.

\#

Grace slept for only an hour, got up to stare blindly at the pill bottles in her bathroom cabinet, opened several, threw down a colorful selection, and blessedly lost consciousness.

#

Logan spent hours going over the cold case file. He needed to have the details down solid before he talked to her. Didn't want to come off as dense or insensitive, just wanted a chance to solve it. He felt as if he owed her somehow and that, in itself, was stupid. He didn't owe her anything. But something behind those golden eyes and her subconscious plea told him this was more than important. And he was used to following his instincts.

Nancy stuck her head into the conference room. "It's eight o'clock. Call it a night detective. Get some sleep."

"I ever mention that I tried to strangle my ex 'cause she nagged all the time? Settled for a divorce, but sometimes I still get itchy fingers."

Nancy laughed. "I could pull rank and order you out of the building."

"Yeah, but you won't. People like you hold a trump card right until the last second. Afraid to waste it just in case the perfect opportunity comes along."

Her eyebrows went up. "You play bridge?"

"Nope. Game called nine-five-two got me through the boredom of high school."

"Huh. I don't remember high school."

He grinned. "Me neither. Just the card games."

"Go home, Logan. Get some sleep. You'll need to

be on your toes when you meet Grace tomorrow. She'll be rested up and ready for you."

"I've survived her under the worst of circumstances twice already and come out alive." He waited a beat. "Bruised but alive."

Nancy laughed. "Walk me to my car, Agent Logan."

"Why, you sweet manipulator, you." He winked, stuffed the file folders into his briefcase, grabbed his battered leather jacket off the back of the chair, flicked the light switch, and followed her to the elevator.

#

It was nine in the morning and Logan had just set up his case board in a conference room. Sure would be nice to have an office again. Not that field work wasn't interesting, but sometimes he missed having everything he needed at his fingertips. He was staring at the facts before him when he heard the door open behind him. "Go away."

"No," Grace replied indignantly.

He swung around quickly. "Sorry. I thought you were someone else."

"Everyone does."

He frowned. What the hell did that mean? He saw her eyes widen and realized she was staring over his shoulder at the board.

"Shit," he muttered, and reached out to turn her away.

She stood her ground. "Anyone ever tell you you're pushy, Detective?"

He opened his mouth to correct her but caught

himself. He'd leave the facts for another time. "You shouldn't have to see this."

"Why not? I was there, remember? No reason I shouldn't see pictures of myself. I always liked that dress. Never got it back, though. They held it for evidence." She shrugged. "Don't suppose it would have ever come clean. All that blood—" She dragged her gaze away and met his look straight on. "You want to reopen this, why?"

"Somebody got away with murder and I want them caught. It's what I do."

"And as a new boy in homicide, you figure you're smarter than them."

"Than who?"

"The guys who worked this the first time. The names are all there: Rogers, Clarke, Dixon, Ramirez, Johnson." It annoyed her to see his surprise. "You don't think I got to know them all? Hell, I spent more time in this building than at home. Knew them all, worked with them, can probably recite every word you see there. I know the angles, the interviews, the measurements, even the weather and the most popular street drugs that week." She smirked at his expression. "You ever seen this case before?"

He lied. "Once."

"What happened that time?"

"Nothing."

"You didn't want justice for the dead man then? Didn't feel driven to take a murderer off the street?" Her shoulders stayed squared.

No doubt honesty was the only way to deal with her. He'd do the best he could. "I hadn't met you. Hadn't messed with your head in the parking garage."

"Guilt, Detective?"

"Some."

"Let it go. It won't do either of us any good. My past is put away. Isaac is dead, nothing will change that. I've moved on."

"But a killer is walking around out there when he should be in a cage."

"No, a mugger who accidentally killed a man will simply go unpunished by the system." She shook her head at his visible annoyance. "You may be new around here and gung-ho to get all the bad guys, solve the cases, leave no stone unturned, and that's just fine for whatever else comes your way. But this is a cold case, one your co-workers already beat to death. Respect that, would you? Isaac died because he carried a concealed weapon. Poor drug-addicted mugger probably suffers every day because of what happened. He had no intention of killing anyone. Isaac pulled the gun, scared the guy, shot himself in the scuffle. End of story."

He scowled at her. "Your lover dies in your arms and you can forgive the man responsible for his death just like," he snapped his fingers in front of her face, "that?"

Grace held his look as long as she could, then walked toward the door, but stopped before reaching for the handle. Her voice was soft when she said, "He loved me first. I loved him back. I'd never been treated as someone who mattered before. The only man I ever loved died in my arms and that—"she held up her hand, snapped her fingers—"took me years to get over. I don't need it all thrown back in my face now. Please." She sighed. "Just let us both rest in peace."

Bullshit. He wanted to grab her, spin her around, look into her eyes and shout *bullshit.* But he didn't dare. There was something she wasn't saying, and he could feel it right down to his bones. He stepped between her and the door. Waited.

Her face lifted, exposing watery golden eyes. He steeled himself, refused to be played.

"You're hiding something," he said.

She shook her head. "I'm just trying to save a little of myself from your scrutiny. I don't like being examined."

"Someone looks like you ought to be used to men staring."

Disappointed, the heat drained out of her. He could have been a stimulating sparring partner but he was just another man after all.

"One little compliment and you shut down on me?"

"You took all the fun out of it."

"Didn't mean to. We dinosaurs tend to speak before we think sometimes. Let's back up and pretend I'm a blind man who has no idea you're drop-dead gorgeous." His voice became soft and serious. "What's the real reason, Grace? Why don't you want the investigation reopened?"

Logan could almost see her wheels grinding while she struggled with what to tell him. Her poker face was good, but he felt the change, knew she was about to lie to him again.

She appeared to study the wall as though searching for cracks. "It's my mother. She's a somewhat famous entertainer. If you open this thing back up, the bad publicity will fall on her again. I'd prefer to keep her happy. Keeps her away from me."

He couldn't help himself. He reached out, cupped her chin, and tipped her face so she had to meet his eyes again. He came in close—too close—and said, "You're lying to me and that pisses me off. It makes me all the more certain I have to reopen this case."

She stayed very still, defiance in her lioness eyes challenging him to go that one step further and lower his mouth to hers. It was exactly what he wanted to do but wouldn't.

Her eyes suddenly glittered with humor and she taunted, "How's the lip healing, Detective? Did you require stitches?"

He stared back, tempted, waiting for just the tiniest sign that she'd come with him, but she never gave him the satisfaction. Instead, her fingers slid up the front of his shirt, removed a pen from his breast pocket, pulled his hand from her face, and wrote a phone number on his palm. "Call at five." She stepped around him and slipped out the door.

#

Grace's expression skidded from one extreme to another while she outlined the events of the last few days, for Sarah.

"You've certainly been busy. Where do you want to start, Grace? What needs our immediate attention?"

"The Brontosaurus."

"What do you want him to know?"

"The facts about Isaac and me. Then make him back off."

"Why don't you want him to reopen the case?"

She held up her hand. "Not the quick answer. You owe yourself the truth. Think about it very carefully." Sarah frowned. "You were about to dump it on your mother, weren't you? Blame everything on Meredith."

"Not everything, just my fucked-up head." Grace smiled at the grimace on Sarah's face.

"Years of therapy and you still go back to the same old dodge. Obviously, I have failed you."

"If it wasn't for her—" Grace swung an arm to encompass the room—"none of this would be necessary."

Sarah could feel the joking coming to an end so she gently prodded. "Why not just let yourself cry for him? Why put her in the middle of it?"

"It's just—" Grace stared out the window, stewing but refusing to open up.

Sarah changed the subject instead of flogging a dead horse. "Tell me again what happened with this cop."

Grace propped her feet on the ottoman and leaned her head back against the softness of the old chair's cushions. "He flashed his badge and everything went into slow motion. When I was running, I could hear him behind me. I was terrified. The nightmares were all coming true. I couldn't run fast enough, my legs were too heavy, too slow, like trying to run in waist-deep water. He looked so angry when he caught me, but when my knee drove into him, his eyes changed like Isaac's probably had after the gun went off. Shock. Pain. Disbelief. Only... then, he became stronger, not weaker, and I couldn't get away from him. And when he kissed me, it was just his mouth pinning mine as though he wasn't involved. He was using it like a weapon to hold me still and I didn't like the feeling at all."

"Is that why you bit him? To get his attention?"

She frowned thoughtfully. "No. I think it was purely to make him let go, same as I'd have done if it had been his hand over my mouth."

"What about being under the car? How did that make you feel?"

"Curiously detached. Have you ever been under one?"

"Detached from the scene?"

"From him. When he shoved me under the car and let go of me, I felt, oddly isolated.

"Were you afraid?"

"I don't think so."

"How did you feel when Logan came back for you?"

"Relieved for just an instant, and then thoroughly pissed off."

"Why?"

"I'm not sure. I guess because he was looking at me as though I was an aggravation, a nuisance he couldn't wait to pass off to someone else."

"Not used to being brushed off so easily, eh, Grace? Much more comfortable pitching than catching."

Grace opened her mouth to disagree and found herself suddenly grinning. "Nice work, Doc."

"I try."

"I'm feeling much better now. A little self-pity and a touch of self-discovery topped off with a near scolding. Probably about used up my time."

"So what do you want me to tell the detective?"

"Whatever it takes to stop him, but make sure he knows it's off the record."

Chapter 4

Logan stared at the number written on his palm. Pissed he hadn't been able to trace it, but glad it was finally seventeen-hundred, he picked up the landline in his pseudo office, and dialed.

"Hello."

"Detective Logan here. I was given this number by Grace Taylor."

"Yes, she told me you'd be calling. My office is in the Fredmont Building. How soon can you be here?"

His eyebrows went up. "How's twenty minutes?"

"Perfect. Suite 460. You'll have to knock."

Eighteen minutes later, Logan was looking at the directory beside the elevator, hoping for a name to attach to the woman he'd spoken to. But Suite 460 didn't seem to exist. He rode up to the fourth flour and found there was no sign on the door, just numbers. He knocked. It swung open almost immediately and a pretty blonde stepped back to invite him in. "Do you have identification, sir?"

He held out his ID card and she barely glanced at it. "Formality. Thanks."

She closed the door and took him from the tiny

reception area into a room that resembled someone's living room filled with an odd mixture of comfortable furniture.

They sat in sofa chairs facing each other with a coffee table in between.

She watched him as he took in the details of his surroundings. "Where would you like to start, Detective?"

He smiled. "Perhaps it would help if I knew who you were and why Grace gave me your number."

She smiled. "She told you nothing?"

He held up his palm to show her the number written there. "She wrote this and said, 'Call at five.'"

The woman laughed. "I'm Sarah Rideout, Grace's psychologist, and she's instructed me to tell you what you need to know. The facts surrounding the incident."

"So you'll tell me all the reasons why I have to drop the case file-boxes back into the dusty basement. And she expects me to be convinced. You must be good."

"I am." She smiled. "I'm going to answer your questions, however, nothing I say leaves this room. Do you understand, Detective Logan?"

"Completely. For my ears only." He closed the tiny notebook he'd been preparing to write in.

She sat back, and folded her hands together. "Fire away, Detective."

"Why doesn't Grace want me to solve Isaac's murder?"

"Their relationship was private, and she wants to keep it that way."

"Because?"

"Partly because Isaac wasn't her lover. He was

her father."

Well, that surprised the hell out of him, but left him oddly pleased. "She'd rather have the press portray her as a—"

"As the lover of a much older man."

"Why?"

"To protect their history."

"Look, I could go on asking *why* every time you end a sentence until I've dragged the whole story out of you, or to save time and eliminate the annoyance factor, you could simply *tell* me the whole story."

Sarah smiled. "I'm beginning to see her point."

"What exactly does that mean?"

"Do you drink coffee detective?"

"Redundancy at its finest." He smiled back at her.

She took a few minutes to fix them coffee, then told him the story. "Grace was eighteen when she found out who her father was. She'd met Isaac once when she was about ten, but hadn't been told of their relationship. Meredith denied him further access to Grace and he stayed away until she was of legal age."

"Nice woman," Logan said under his breath.

"Meredith has the look of an angel, a voice to die for, a huge following of adoring fans, and a mean streak a mile wide. And, unlike beauty, it's way more than skin deep."

Meredith, the rock star, movie actress, and tabloid queen. In his mind he could see the famous singer, five-foot-nothing, delicate, ivory skin, silvery blonde hair, big blue eyes. He looked at Sarah. "You'd pass for Meredith's daughter long before Grace ever would. They're complete opposites."

Sarah reached for the file folder beside her chair,

pulled out a photo, and handed it to him. It was Isaac and Grace. She was obviously the female image of her father.

Logan let the impressions sink in. Long, lean, golden-eyed. Lion and lioness. Hunters. *Hunters?* He studied the picture, wondering where that word had come from.

Sarah interrupted his thoughts. "Obviously no need for DNA confirmation. They became constant companions. It worked well for them. Grace and Isaac both loved to travel, but she'd found it difficult as a single woman, and society looks suspiciously upon older men holidaying alone. Anyway, they teamed up and had a ball together. He was wealthy enough that they traveled the world for several years, staying in luxury suites and private villas. Then Isaac bought the house for them to share just outside the city, the house Grace still lives in. They had extraordinary privacy there. They both felt safe."

"Safe from what? Who?"

"Meredith. She can be very, ah... demanding sometimes, and Grace has great difficulty standing up to her."

Logan had a hard time believing the Grace who'd kneed him in the nuts had a problem standing up to *anyone*, but he let it slide. "Okay so now I have background, but I don't see any reason not to open the case. What does she think will happen?"

Sarah swung her gaze to the empty sky outside the window, took a deep breath, and let it out slowly. "Grace was glad the case was put away because she didn't want her father's private life dragged through the mud. She wanted his memory left alone. She honored who he was, how he loved her, the sacrifices he made for her. She loved him. She'd never had parental love before and it was something she'd craved.

"As it stands, he belongs to her in memory. If it gets into the light, others will take him away from her by smearing his goodness and exposing his secrets. She is simply protecting herself and Isaac—afraid the media will get wind of the investigation and turn it into a circus."

He studied the woman sitting across from him, wondering why she was lying. He changed the subject abruptly with, "Is Grace on medication?"

She blinked. "No."

"Do you think she's getting meds from her physician?"

"For what?"

"Depression? Anxiety? Migraines?"

"Possibly migraines, she doesn't suffer from depression or anxiety. If she did, I'd be the one advising medication."

"So she has headaches?"

"Used to, when she lived with Meredith."

"Ah, ditch the wicked mother and the pain goes away."

"Better interpretation: remove yourself from the triggers and the headaches won't happen."

He smiled suddenly. "Mine was more interesting."

"Colorful."

"And accurate. As her psychologist, do you think it will be harmful to Grace if I re-open the case?"

"Only if the media get their teeth into it."

He grimaced. "I can't guarantee they won't."

"Then yes, it will be potentially harmful to my patient's peace of mind."

"Purely because someone may learn that Isaac was her father and not her lover? People would stop thinking of her as a gold-digger and see her as a loving daughter. *That* would be harmful to her because—?"

"It would point to Meredith. A piece of her not-so-nice past revealed, and she'd take it out on Grace."

"And Grace has reason to fear her mother?" His eyes held hers and dared her to lie to him.

"Yes."

"And that's all you're going to tell me."

"Yes again, Detective."

"Okay." He recognized a brick wall when his forehead was up against it. "I'll leave now, but may I come back?"

"Perhaps." The message in her smile was clear: it would be up to Grace.

"May I ask if your patient is still in therapy?"

"You may ask..." The smile moved up into her eyes. "Her."

He stood and held out his hand. "Thank you for your candor. I'll see myself out."

She held up a key and said quietly, "Not without this."

Logan laughed. "You lock your patients in?"

"Sometimes." She twisted the key in the lock. "It's been a pleasure meeting you, Detective, finding out that you're intense but not quite the bully, I'd envisioned.

\#

45

Logan planted himself in front of Nancy. "I *need* to talk to her."

"Not until you tell me why."

"I promised she'd be the first to know."

"Wrong why. I want to know why you're going to open the case?"

He shook his head. "I can't give you a definitive answer. All I can say is, I have to follow my gut feeling. My subconscious is picking up something I need to explore."

"Would you drop it if I asked you to do it for me?"

"Not unless you can give me a damn good reason that doesn't include the emotional well-being of one long-legged, bad-tempered woman."

"I suggest you seriously explore that emotional state before you take another step forward."

"I would if I could find her."

"She's likely gone to Paradise." As he raised both hands to mockingly reach for her throat she laughed. "No really. It's an exclusive country inn. She goes there to ride. Horses." She glanced at her watch. "You could make it by noon if you left now."

"And how the devil do I get to Paradise?"

Nancy's attempt to choke down the laugh failed.

Logan stuffed his hands in his pockets. "I can't believe you made me say that." Her laughter continued in spite of his scowl. "Don't even think of telling me to take a left at the Pearly Gates or I *will* throttle you with my bare hands."

Nancy wiped tears from her cheeks. "You should have seen your face." A couple more chuckles escaped. "You're way too serious these days, Logan.

Take a drive to Paradise and lighten up." Laughter rolled out of her again.

Smiling now, he shook his head. "You're a wicked woman. Do you pull the wings off flies, too?"

"Aw come on. I'm just having a little fun here. Don't get mad."

He grinned. "You know my rules: never get mad, always get even. So watch your back, woman."

"No threats or I won't give you what you want." She winked.

"What, no more wild sex on your desk? Come on, Nance. That's not fair to either of us."

She chuckled. "Oh, you're a bad one." Her phone rang then and the moment of foolishness ended. She scribbled directions on a piece of paper and passed it to Logan.

He saluted and headed for his car.

Nancy's phone call was nothing important, but the one she'd make next was. Logan wouldn't be happy if he found out, but she had a responsibility.

\#

Logan was just about to get into his car when his cell phone vibrated. He dug it from his pocket and glanced at the symbol. Shit. "Sir."

"Logan. My office."

He glanced up at the window of Nancy's office. He didn't believe in coincidence. He'd bet his favorite ball cap she'd tossed this roadblock in his path. "I'm in the field, Chief."

"If I have your completed report on my desk why are you still in the field?"

Climbing into his car he said, "I've stumbled onto something I think we should look into."

"I sent you there for a job. It's done. I need you back here."

The lack of steel in his superior's voice convinced Logan to work it. "Respectfully, sir, I think this situation is worth investigating."

"What is it?"

"If you give me twenty-four hours, I'll present you with a complete rundown."

"I need you somewhere else."

"My gut's telling me you'll want this one, too."

"Jesus, Logan. You're pushing the boundaries. Again."

His gut clutched. He could hear the pendulum swing. "I know, sir, but I think it's worth it. Eighteen hours?"

"Tomorrow. My office. Oh-seven-hundred."

Chapter 5

Logan drove alongside an eight-foot stone wall for what felt like a mile before pulling up to an ornate black wrought iron gate. The word *Paradise* engraved in a brass plate was barely visible over the tiny speaker box embedded in a stone pillar to his left. He rolled down the window and a tinny voice asked for his name and the reason for his visit.

"I'm here to see Grace Taylor. My name is Logan."

"Just a moment please, sir."

He waited, taking in a view of little more than grass, trees, and pavement. The tinny voice came back, telling him to follow the main driveway and the signs for stable parking. He would be met shortly.

The gates swung open.

Once he'd driven past the trees lining the entrance, he slowed to get a good look at his surroundings. The place was quite spectacular, rather like Kentucky horse country. Acres of rolling hills, miles of black fences, modern barns with slate roofs and copper weathervanes, horses everywhere, and no manure to be seen.

Getting out of his car in the immaculate

49

cobblestoned yard, he caught movement and color to his left. Four young women on horseback, each wearing a puffy, bright red vest, emerged from a bridle path. Just as he decided Grace wasn't among them, another woman stepped out of the nearest barn and approached him with a professional smile in place.

"Welcome to Paradise, Mr. Logan. Grace is almost finished. She'll be with you in a few minutes." She switched her attention to the group of riders. "Did you have a good ride, girls?"

Only one spoke, her voice very low and accented. "It was a lovely ride, thank you, Caroline. It is such a fine day to be outdoors."

The other three nodded, keeping their attention firmly on the older woman, not so much as sparing him a glance.

"I'm glad you enjoyed yourselves," Caroline said. "After you've rubbed them down, don't forget to put boots and rugs on your horses before turning them out in their paddocks."

He was surprised guests were expected to look after the horses at such an exclusive place. He would have expected them to step off, hand the reins to a groom, and walk away. Interesting.

"Feel free to look around, Mr. Logan. Wander if you wish. Grace shouldn't be long." Caroline left him there.

He studied the lay-out. Three barns, an indoor arena, an outdoor ring, and a round building he figured housed a training mill. There were about twenty large turnout paddocks, double-fenced, each with a shelter.

Sudden awareness of Grace's presence had him searching until he caught sight of her nearly a city block away, pushing a wheelbarrow. As she approached, he was surprised to realize that, with faded jeans stuffed into gumboots, an oversized work shirt, hair pulled into a single braid, and heavy leather gloves hiding the long fingers, she was still unmistakably elegant.

She left her equipment in a shed and walked straight toward him, not stopping until she was slightly closer than necessary, just inside his personal space, feet apart, arms crossed, and her amber eyes glinting with amusement.

That threw him. Her body language said *ready to fight* yet he'd have sworn she was trying hard not to laugh.

"What do you want from me now, Logan?"

"Same thing as before. Truth."

"And you always get what you want?"

"Yep."

"Well then, Detective, this will be a new experience for you." Her jaw clenched as though fighting to keep the smile at bay. "You're not going to get what you want."

"Why's that?"

"My life, my decision. Bug off."

"It could get ugly."

"I've been to ugly and lived through it." She flicked the edge of his jacket aside to expose the leather strap of his shoulder holster. "So nothing you can do will scare me. Lock me up and shove bamboo shoots under my nails if you must, but I'm still not talking."

Now he was sure. "I bet Chinese water torture would make you fold."

"No sir, it wouldn't." She sighed and fluttered her eyelashes ever so slightly. "Unless you've got a good old-fashion rack in your basement, you've got no shot."

She stood so close he could feel her warm breath on his face. "A rack, you say." His lips twitched. "That could be arranged. I'd have to send in your measurements though. You're way too tall for the standard model."

He edged back just a bit, gave her a studied glance from head to toe, then back again. "Not often I meet a woman can almost look me in the eye."

"It's not often I meet a man and can't see the top of his head," she countered, smirking. "Of course, I do know how to make you bend over quickly."

"And did the top of my head pass inspection?" he asked with narrowed eyes.

"Noticed a couple of gray hairs."

"You did not."

"Maybe I should take another look."

He felt the impulse even before the subtle movement, the shifting of her weight to one foot. He took a half step to one side and said quietly, "If I go down, you're going with me this time, lady. Ever had a horse manure face wash?"

"Well, well, you do have a ruthless streak." The sudden grin she aimed at him made something move in his chest.

He blinked. "My God, you *can* smile."

"Amazing, eh?" She shrugged and moved away from him, headed for the stable doorway. "Coffee's on in the tack-room if you want it, I'll be right back."

The moment he stepped inside, the high

frequency and electricity of a very thorough security system vibrated through his body. He glanced around. One corner of the spacious room was set up as an office, complete with desk and filing cabinet. Logan circled several couches and chairs to reach the kitchenette in the far corner and poured himself a coffee, then feigned interest in the photographs on the vast wall of folding doors while he concentrated on the swirling energy.

He located four microphones and two cameras. Nothing in this room would be private. His interest piqued, he wandered out, and down the aisle between box stalls, mentally mapping the electronics his senses picked up. A microphone at every stall, a camera at every fourth. That'd be about fifty feet apart for video feed, audio every twelve.

A big black horse watching his approach nickered softly and Logan smiled. "Hello there, big guy." He offered his hand, palm up, and it was carefully checked out before the horse lifted his head, looked past him, and let out a series of happy nickers. Glancing back, Logan was surprised to see Grace had come up behind him. He hadn't felt her presence. Must be all the electronics screwing with his senses.

"I see you've met the most important man in my life."

"You talkin' to the horse or me?"

"Cute." She extended a hand toward the magnificent beast and waited as he gently lipped a peppermint from her palm. "This is Farley, the love of my life."

"Comic strip or author?"

"Pardon?"

"*Farley* for the big awkward comic strip dog, or for the author of the *Black Stallion*?"

She tipped her head at him. "The author, of course. I grew up worshiping him. I take it you read the books?"

"Every last one, *Alex* was my hero."

"Amazing."

"Why?"

"We have so much in common. Would you prefer to walk or ride?"

Startled by the offer to ride, he looked at his slacks and shoes. "Not exactly dressed to ride."

"Come on." She led him back into the tack room and opened a large cupboard. "Guests at the inn often don't have riding clothes with them." Labeled shelves contained a huge selection of jeans, breeches, chaps, boots, and leggings.

While he chose jeans, chaps, and boots for himself, she opened another door, exchanged her big jacket for a puffy red vest and her gumboots for paddock boots.

He nearly swallowed his tongue when, over his shoulder, he caught the rear view of her bent over, zipping herself into butter-soft gray leather chaps. He must have made some kind of sound because she said, "Changing room's the first door on the left. I'll get us a couple of horses."

Chapter 6

The trail she chose wasn't wide enough for riding side-by-side so few words passed between them while she led the way. For half an hour he watched her body move, her hips swaying with the movement of the horse. She was supple, graceful, elegant, and very still in the tack. Arriving at a clearing beside a small lake, they dismounted and clipped the horses to a tether-line between two trees. They left their helmets hooked to their saddles.

"Are we safe here?" he asked.

She stared at him. "What do you mean by that?"

"No prying eyes?"

Grace frowned and walked away from him to stand at the water's edge and stare off into the distance.

He followed and put his hands on her shoulders—only to jerk back from a jolt of energy. The vest was wired. He guessed it would be a listening device in the collar, close to her mouth.

When she turned to look at him with a question in her eyes, he held a finger to his mouth, then gambled. Moving his hands slowly in sign, he was rewarded by her fingers signaling her understanding and agreement.

He unzipped the vest and keeping his words soft, yet clear, said, "I've been waiting for days to get your clothes off."

She rolled her eyes and laughed nervously. "So your patience with me has been a ruse?"

He smiled, slipped his arms under the vest and whispered in her ear, "The patience was real, my love, but it didn't make the longing any less intense." He pushed the vest from her shoulders and let it drop to the ground.

"Logan?"

"Come with me."

He held onto her hand and led her into the trees, away from the water and the horses. They walked in silence for about a hundred yards. "I need to be sure," he said reaching out to touch her. "May I?" At her nod, he steeled himself against the feel of her body while running his hands from the top of her head to the soles of her boots. He stood back with a satisfied smile. "All clear."

"And you're about a whisker away from a slap to your smug face." Her expression was mutinous.

"Did you already know you were wired?" he asked, just a shade confused.

She didn't hesitate. "No."

"So you're mad because I knew before you?"

"No. I'm annoyed you think you have the right to put your hands on me."

"Grace, I was checking for devices. I'm a professional."

Her sudden grin caught him off guard. "So does that mean you haven't been pining for me? You weren't serious about getting my clothes off?"

He caught up quick. "Well, there's a little truth in every lie, but I'm not about to divulge my secrets."

She switched back to serious in a heartbeat. "How did you know about the microphone?"

Logan was surprised, but didn't hesitate to tell her the truth. "I have a feeling for the energy."

"It could have been a phone in my pocket."

He nodded. "True, but my senses are specifically tuned to certain types of frequencies. And I'd already noticed the stable air bloody crackling with it—more stuff in there than in the White House. Seemed a bit odd. Put me on edge." He studied her face, wondering what kind of explanation she'd come up with.

"It's a very long story."

He led her toward a fallen tree so they could sit. "I've got all the time in the world."

Grace closed her eyes to steady herself for a moment while establishing a clear picture in her mind.

"Pay attention, Detective. This is the condensed version. Isaac's mother, my grandmother, was Katarina Petrovna, a world-famous prima ballerina from a small Eastern European country. She attracted the interest of a prince, had a torrid affair, and ended up pregnant. When his wife intercepted a message from Katarina to the prince, the woman intervened and made a deal Katarina couldn't resist. With a large sum of money in hand, she defected to the States so her unborn child, an illegitimate heir to the throne, would remain a secret.

"In America, after Isaac's birth, Katarina made no effort to hide and went back to the Ballet, headlining in major productions for years. She eventually retired very wealthy and highly respected. Isaac, from birth, was groomed to be a dancer, but genetics prevented a serious career. His father, the prince, had been well over six feet tall and Isaac didn't stop growing until he was six-foot-four, and far too tall for the classic stage."

Grace stopped for a moment and shivered. Logan took off his jacket and put it around her. She gave him a vague smile and continued, "When he was in university, he danced in many dramatic productions and music videos, much to Katarina's disdain. But that's how he came to meet my mother. Meredith had—has—a thing for dancers. She collects them, uses them, then tosses them away, always looking for a new one. It's her signature and she flaunts it. She's been quoted saying things like, 'Any man who can control his body so exquisitely makes an incredible lover,' or 'Dancers are sensitive to their partners' needs,' and 'They have stamina and athleticism combined with grace and agility.'" She grimaced. "A gossip rag even dragged me into it once. *Like mother like daughter,* was printed under a picture of me dancing with Isaac. It was followed by a juicy tale of my wild escapades."

He couldn't help himself from asking since she was so serious. "And is it true, Grace?" He ran a finger down her cheek. "Does it take the stamina of a dancer to please you?"

She shoved him off the log. He lay on his back laughing at the indignant look on her face.

She glowered at him for a full minute before saying, "You really are asking for it, Logan."

"Asking for what?"

"A damn fine slap, and I'm just the woman to give it to you." Her sudden grin was laced with wickedness. "I could have you beheaded."

"Okay, princess, but help me up first, okay?"

She avoided his hand and grabbed his wrist instead. She pulled him up for just a second, then let go, laughing as he fell back. But the laugh turned into a startled squeak when he was suddenly on his feet behind her with a hand locked in her hair.

Grace sobered and stared into the dark blue eyes above her.

His voice was husky soft as he watched her expression. "Cat got your tongue, beautiful?"

"Let go of my hair, Brontosaurus," she whispered.

"It'll cost ya." He dipped his head and almost grazed her lips, tickling her with the words, "Dinosaurs have lousy manners." He stuffed his hands into his pockets, then sat down beside her and said quietly, "Go on with your story."

She took a deep breath. "When Meredith kicked Isaac to the curb, he took off to Europe for a while. That's when it got complicated. Katarina died, and her death made headlines. Especially when her son's age was noted in her home country and someone, somewhere, connected the dots. Voilà, the royal family learned of his existence. His father confirmed the rumors about an affair with Katarina and Isaac was accepted as his father's only male child. He stayed in the palace for a few years, but eventually became unhappy with the situation, feeling like a fraud. He began to travel a lot and returned to America where he fell in love with a man. He led a secret, double life—in the closet both as a gay man and as a prince."

She dug her fingers into the tight muscles across the top of her shoulders. "When I met Isaac on my eighteenth birthday, he explained his concern about his royal-and-not-very-nice family becoming a problem for me. So we decided to keep our relationship a secret as well. As long as no one ever knew I was his daughter, I was safe."

Her mouth quirked with the hint of a smile. "When we attended one of Meredith's events together, a picture of us dancing made it into a tabloid. We were then linked as a couple, providing us the cover we needed. It was actually fun pretending we were lovers. Our very own joke on the world. But the night he died, someone, somehow, heard me plead with my 'papa' not to leave me. I was approached shortly afterwards and have been under the protection of their government ever since. They scaled back the security in several areas after I threatened to go public about the affair with Katarina, however, lately, since you've been picking at the case file, the security has been tightened again."

"Why? Why would that make a difference?"

"Your digging around could expose my identity."

"And why is that a problem?"

She shrugged. "I don't know exactly. I'm just told it would be dangerous."

"How does your mother feel about all of this?"

She laughed wryly. "My mother knows nothing."

"Nothing at all?"

She didn't want to go on with this. His questions could eventually trip her up. "Nothing aside from Isaac being my father, that he died in a mugging, and, unfortunately, the press ran some lousy pictures of her daughter at the scene of the crime. She's never forgiven me for allowing those photographs to be taken. You know, smudged makeup, dress all askew, blood on my hands, my hair a mess..." A shudder ran through her.

Logan dropped an arm around her shoulders and she leaned her head against him. "I had nightmares for weeks about that blood. I could never get it off of my hands."

He stroked her hair and she sighed. "It's getting late. We'd better head back soon or they'll get worried."

He smirked. "Perhaps they'll think I have the stamina of a dancer."

She looked into his smiling face and shook her head. "I'm sure I'll regret ever saying those things to you."

He kept his eyes fixed on hers as he lowered his head and kissed her ever so gently. "I will only use your own words against you when I'm sure you need to hear them."

"Logan?"

His mouth had moved across her throat, tasting, savoring. "Hmmm?"

Her heart was pounding way too fast. "Stop that."

"Why?"

Warmth spread through her, her body becoming traitor to her mind. She had to stop. She couldn't afford to let him keep touching her. Her jaw tightened and she opened her eyes to stare at him. "We have to leave now."

"Why?"

"Because I am *not* going to get naked with you out here."

He stared at her, looking genuinely surprised. "I

don't recall asking you to."

"If you don't pocket those talented lips pretty darn quick there won't be time for asking."

"You playing me, Grace?" His eyes challenged her.

Oh yeah, she thought, hooking a finger in his collar and drawing him forward until her lips feathered over his. "I'm a dancer, too, Detective, and sometimes I like to lead." Her mouth opened, moving hungrily under his.

Logan took advantage, took control, sliding his fingers into her hair and holding her still while he plundered the dark heat of her mouth and the fire built. Her hands slipped under his sweater and a purring sound rose from her throat as her long, sensitive fingers explored his muscular chest.

He finally tore free and stared down at her. "What the hell am I doing?" he muttered.

"Sweating, Detective."

His eyes narrowed. "Excuse me?"

She made sure he saw she was fighting a smile. "You're trying to decide if you dare have sex with me. Trying to rationalize and figure out how badly it will screw up the case."

"Is that what you're up to? Distracting me from why I came here?"

Calculating feline eyes searched his. "Why *are* you here, Detective?"

"I came to tell you I'm going ahead with my investigation. I'm going to find Isaac's murderer." He hesitated. "Unless you can convince me otherwise."

"And have I convinced you yet?"

"No."

With a faint, shadowy smile, and a smoky voice she said, "Perhaps I should take you dancing."

Logan chose to ignore the innuendo. "Perhaps we should get back on the horses."

Abruptly, she shrugged and walked away. He followed, unable to take his eyes off her. She even walked like a lioness, her movements unconscious yet magnificent. Genetically programed, grace.

He could imagine her on stage, an audience in the palm of her hand, while she became the music, and the thought slipped softly from his lips, "Born to dance."

She stopped dead in her tracks.

The fluid curve of her spine stiffened and her shoulders pulled back as though he'd put the barrel of a gun between them.

And while he sensed a fissure and vulnerability, when she spun to face him ice dripped from her tongue as she snarled, "Don't *ever* say that again."

He reached for her. "Why?"

Grace shied away from his touch. "Please..." She hesitated, knowing her reaction was unreasonable but unable to stop it. "Just don't."

She turned her back on him and wondered how the hell she could make such a mistake after being so careful. She'd stayed within her plan, saying only what she'd wanted to, allowing nothing to slip, keeping her guard up. Until now.

They rode back in silence. Grace stewed for a while, fully conscious of the eyes fastened on her back, well aware of him studying her as the horses carried them through the woods. She paid little attention to the scenery, the crisp freshness of the air, the lovely warmth of sunshine filtering through the trees. She knew her slip had been noted. How far would he research? How deep would he dig? She swallowed hard. She'd have to work him some more, make him forget that tiny flaw in her picture. Make him shove it aside as temperamental, inconsequential.

The path widened as they approached the stables, and he nudged his horse alongside hers. "You know, if we supposedly just spent the afternoon, ah, *together*, you should probably ditch the scowl. Someone may get the wrong impression. Doubt my stamina."

She slid a sideways look at him and laughed softly. "How'd you like to go dancing tonight, Detective?"

Logan was cautious about her meaning. "Where exactly?"

"The local country club."

"Maybe another time I have no suitable clothes with me."

"We could stay here then. The inn has a lovely dance floor in the solarium."

He took in the challenge, the golden sparkle in her eyes, and felt her dare as distinctly as fingernails gliding down his back, teasing, threatening to dig in. It would be a mistake to dance with her. She was trying to bait him enough that he'd take her up on it as a game but she'd win. Just the thought of her moving to music in his arms tightened the knot in his belly. He wasn't willing to gamble with the invitation she threatened to hand him. The woman was trouble and he knew it as certainly as she knew he did. He couldn't afford the distraction.

Could he?

Chapter 7

Caroline stepped out of the barn and took their horses, saying she'd put them away, then winked at Grace. "I sent Logan's clothes up to your place. Thought he'd rather change there."

Her place? Logan played along, looking back and forth between them, then shrugged and dropped an arm around Grace's shoulders. "Point me."

"My car's parked down at the kennel. We'll take yours." Grace said.

Following her directions, he'd driven about half a mile in the opposite direction from where they'd ridden when he spotted the house. A low wooden structure with enormous windows nestled among the trees on a hill overlooking the wide expanse of property.

When he walked through the back entrance into the great room, the view through all that glass was incredible. The mixed landscape of groomed pastures and treed wilderness was expected, but the glimpse of what looked like a Scottish castle was a surprise. "*That's* the inn?"

"The heart and soul of Paradise."

"Impressive. How many people at capacity?"

"Good question."

"You don't know?"

"We've never experienced capacity."

He didn't miss her use of the word *we*. Did she live here? Work here? Run the stables? He shook his head, frustrated by her tactics yet unwilling to ask her outright. Instead, he continued along the same vein of inquiry. "How many guestrooms are there?"

"Well, we have five suites, each with at least three bedrooms. And the upper floor is a single suite with seven bedrooms."

"A *seven* bedroom suite? Who needs seven bedrooms?"

"We cater to royalty and diplomatic dignitaries—the kind of folk who travel with an entourage." She smiled. "We once had a prince and his wife on the top floor with their three children, a nanny, and a domestic aide. Two personal assistants, four body guards, and two drivers stayed in three other suites." She tossed him a curious look. "Didn't you investigate Paradise before you drove out?"

Now he felt like a damned idiot and it didn't sit well. He was good at what he did. Shit didn't get by him. Women didn't screw with his instincts or his job. Until now. "I was pretty damned irritated when you wouldn't return my calls so I cornered Nancy this morning and she said you'd probably come here to ride. Gave me directions."

"This is one of a collection of properties Isaac liked to call his sanctuaries. Living as a prince for a while, he experienced some of the difficulties and lack of privacy encountered by those who cannot simply stroll into a hotel—for whatever reason."

"How many inns?" He went for blunt.

But her answer was evasive. "I run a rather large enterprise from afar."

"This looks pretty close up to me."

"Not really. I indulge myself by working in the stables several days a week and riding as often as I choose. I hate being trapped indoors. Office work would drive me to insanity for sure. I have an excellent staff. Isaac's. People I can depend on to keep the business in order."

He let her words sink in while he studied the room where they stood. Comfortable, lots of leather and wood mixed with light colors, but nothing personal. More like a high-end furnished residence than a personal home. No female imprint of ownership, no nesting. The place could belong to anyone.

But the floor caught his interest. He'd bet his pay-check it was reclaimed from an old building. Polished plank oak with a history. Logan had a thing about old wooden floors. He loved to speculate about the hundreds of thousands of footsteps they'd felt. Too bad the floor, the only connection to history, didn't speak of the woman who owned it but of faceless others from nameless places.

Frowning at his thoughts, he followed Grace when she gestured him toward a hallway that led to what appeared to be the only bedroom, where his slacks were neatly laid out.

Her voice was soft, almost wistful, when she asked, "Would you like a shower first?"

He missed none of the meaning in her words and answered with care, "Another time. I need to get back to town."

She appeared to understand the game had come to an end, but left the door slightly ajar. He exchanged the borrowed jeans and boots for his own pants and shoes as he scrutinized the room.

While reasonably feminine, it didn't speak of her and her scent vanished quickly, as though it didn't belong.

The agent in him made mental notes: nothing extra on the surfaces, no brush or comb on the dresser, only a simple clock radio on the nightstand.

In the bathroom, he opened the medicine cabinet to find only a toothbrush and paste. The shower stall had a single bar of soap, unused, a bottle of drug store shampoo, and a tiny bristled brush. To clean the stable dirt from under her nails, he supposed. Towels were fluffy and showed little wear, the robe hanging behind the door was thick and expensive. Opening the cabinet beneath the sink, he found three rolls of toilet paper, and one box of tampons, unopened.

Back in the bedroom, he took a quick look in the closet, expecting it to be empty. He was surprised. There were five neatly arranged outfits rather like the one she'd put on when they'd woken her the morning after the parking garage incident, and about a half dozen floor length dresses.

He'd just counted fourteen pairs of shoes lined up on a shelf when he felt a warning tingle and stepped away from the closet as she entered the room.

"Find anything you like?" she asked.

"Nothing in my size, thanks." He gave her a look that said *I'm a cop, what the hell did you expect?'*

She shrugged, her face a mask of indifference, as though his searching was exactly what she'd expected.

They parted quickly then, politely, as strangers would. She declined his offer of a ride back to the stables where her car was. Said she could use the walk.

He didn't want to leave, but knew he had to. He cruised the winding roadway and passed the fancy gate with the weight of apprehension chewing at his gut.

#

After making a few phone calls, Grace hiked to the kennels near the inn to retrieve Milo. Poor guy hated lock-up, but being something of a twit when it came to his own safety, he couldn't be trusted around the horses. In spite of being kicked once, he still stupidly snapped at the heels of any passing horse.

Now, he hopped about barking, thrilled that she'd come back for him, as though worried that one day she wouldn't. "Time to go home, silly dog."

Caroline flagged her down as she drove past the stables. "You didn't ride Farley. Want me to turn him out?"

Grace groaned, annoyed with herself for being so preoccupied. She could put Milo back in the kennel now and take Farley out for a ride, but her heart wouldn't be in it.

"Would you mind putting him on the training mill for a half hour first? Just a standard walk, trot, canter. Then he can have a couple of hours outside."

"Dressed?" asked Caroline.

Grace glanced up at the sky and squinted. "The sun's pretty warm today, so take his rug off, but put his bell-boots on."

"Got it," Caroline said. "Quinn called earlier."

Grace's stomach clutched at the familiar announcement. "How did he sound?"

"Upbeat as always. Says he expects to hear from Rachel soon. Feels it in his gut."

"The man is half lunatic, half saint, and stupid in love." Grace shook her head. "I sure couldn't spend my days counseling PTSD patients, and my nights running searches in hope of finding my runaway wife."

"He loves her and understands why she had to disappear." She shrugged. "Speaking of disappearing," she said with a cheeky smile. "How'd you let that good-looking cop get away so quick?"

"What makes you think he's a cop?"

Caroline laughed. "Two things about the guy that were a very easy read. Number one, he's a cop. Number two, he wants you. Oh yeah, and he's got a great ass. Noticed that, too."

Grace smirked. "You're very observant."

"I can't believe you sent him away. Man was yours, skin, bone, muscles, the whole handsome package." She cocked her head. "It's not like you to play games, Grace."

"Good point, but I don't want to talk about him." She ran her hand over Milo's head and down his back.

"You coming out tomorrow?"

Grace pursed her lips while she thought about it. "If I'm not here by ten, assume I'm not coming and kick Farley out for the day."

"Yes, ma'am." Caroline chuckled. "If you're not here by ten, can I at least fantasize that you decided to put the cop out of his misery?"

Grace shook her head and managed an indignant

frown. "You're awful."

"Don't begrudge me a little vicarious pleasure. Sergei's had three back-to-back assignments, sure would like a tumble soon."

Grace wasn't fooled by the flippant remark. Being married to an undercover operative had to be hard. "When's he due home?"

"Twenty-two more nights of loneliness," Caroline said with a sigh.

"Good thing you're not counting."

#

The return drive to the city was old. Grace did it about five days a week so there was little to capture her interest. She drove as though on auto-pilot while her mind flew back to the hours she'd spent with Logan. She didn't try to kid herself about the attraction. The man's touch made her forget herself. Forget the rules. That alone should make him off-limits.

Was she making a mistake even talking to him? Somewhere in her head she knew she was, yet in her gut... There was something else. Could she trust him with the truth? Did she dare take that chance?

Fairly certain he hadn't missed anything today, even her one slip, there was nothing she could do now but wait. Two days, tops.

But she'd give him three.

Chapter 8

Logan's visit to Paradise had been far less successful than he'd planned. Hoping to gain insight when Grace's guard was down, he'd allowed her to choreograph their performance and manipulate their interaction. But there was a great deal more going on with her than he'd expected and she had iron control over her thoughts.

He ran through the day, scene by scene, as he drove back to the station and found his determination to investigate her father's murder now coupled with his need to know what else was going on with her. Why the complex games? Why the need to control the interpretation of every observed nuance between her and an over-eager homicide detective?

Logan parked in front of the building, eager to get his observations on paper, to see the balance and better weigh the inconsistencies, but Nancy was waiting for him when he stepped off the elevator.

"My office," she said and walked away.

He followed as she obviously expected him to, but protested with, "Kind of in a hurry, Nance."

She pointed to the couch as she settled behind her desk. "Sit. Tell me about your trip to Paradise."

He stayed standing, ran a hand through his hair. "It was interesting."

She lifted a single eyebrow. "And what does that mean?"

"It's an amazing property."

"Did you get her to talk about Isaac's murder?"

He let out a frustrated half laugh. "No. But I did get some background on him and his family. Details for the big picture."

"And?" she prompted.

Annoyance gnawed at him. He strapped it down. Cut to the chase. "She's seems hell-bent on seducing me."

"Making any headway?"

"No. Yes. Dammit, she's enough woman to keep a guy warm for a decade or two, but she's only trying to distract me."

Nancy wasn't sure if she should grin or grimace. "With some success I'd say. You look like a man with a problem."

He headed for the door. "Just beat. Long day, long drive, lots of tidbits to piece together and analyze." He winked at her. "Nothing a cold shower won't cure.

He was already gone when she said quietly into the empty air, "I wouldn't count on it."

#

Once Logan finished the detailed notes about his trip to Paradise, he sat back and read through the cold case file again, hoping with his new insight, something might read differently, stir up a question for him to work on, an angle to explore.

But nothing new popped. In fact, each time he went through the file, he realized just how little useful information it contained. He'd expected a dozen boxes of evidence and data after Grace had listed names as though there'd been a task force involved. Turned out, they were all part of the immediate investigation, the one at the crime scene. But the file had been handled by a single detective who concentrated on harassing the homeless in search of the perpetrator. And there wasn't a single follow-up interview with Grace. Or anyone else, for that matter.

He closed up the conference room, drove to the hotel, picked up his messages and dirty laundry, got back into his car, then hit the highway—for home.

Six hours later, sitting at his desk, the one wedged into a corner of the living room, he googled Isaac Petrovna, and came up with absolutely nothing. When he accessed the agency databases, again he found nothing more than a birth certificate and Social Security number. There was no record of Isaac being attached to any European royal family. No official documentation had ever existed on the man.

Way too clean.

Logan leaned back in his chair, tapping fingertips on the edge of the desk. Her story had sounded real, but his radar had been flickering, warning him of a lie. And the facts weren't coming together as she'd told them; there were fragments of information sending up flags.

She'd said someone had heard her plead with her "papa" not to die. *Someone*? There had been no witnesses. But there was a photograph. Who had taken it, sold it to the rags? Isaac was supposed to be a university graduate yet there was no record of a degree. Was she really being monitored by a foreign country? Why? And why exactly would a man like Isaac be carrying a concealed weapon? Had he not been at a social event? Wearing a tuxedo? In a highly secure building within the diplomatic circle? Diplomatic circle. A place where...

He picked up the landline, punched buttons, and waited for the beep.

"Call me, I'm at a dead end, but I *know* the street goes through."

Logan went to the kitchen poured himself another cup of cold coffee, nuked it too long, cursed, dropped in an ice cube, and sat back at the desk as the phone rang. He smiled—hadn't lost his timing anyway. "Hey, Brad."

"Why are you picking my brain at this hour?"

"Can't sleep 'cause somethin's buggin' me."

"So it makes perfect sense to ruin my sleep, too?"

He glanced at the clock. Midnight. "Shit. I didn't even look at the time. Sorry, man. Go back to bed. Call me in the morning."

"Guilt's good, thanks. Okay, so I wasn't asleep yet. Whatcha got?"

Logan gave him nothing but names. Brad preferred it that way. He would do a clean search without bias.

"Is this a rush?"

"Not urgent, but as soon as you can. There's something about it that's bugging me."

"So you said."

"Go back to bed, Brad, and kiss Cheryl for me."

"Get your own woman."

#

Logan parked below a nondescript ten-story building tucked amid a cluster of office towers, and used a fob to access the elevator. Once inside, he stepped up to the iris scanner and waited for a blinking green light before selecting the eighth floor. The other nine floors were occupied by offices of Interpol, FBI, CIA, CISIS, Scotland Yard, and covert agencies, all under the guise of a chemical research facility.

He stepped off the elevator into the mantrap, where he waited to be cleared into the offices of ETC—officially called Etcetera because they encompassed everything *else*. A diverse bunch of individuals ranging from telepaths and animal behaviorists to cat-burglars and scientists, serving the world in ways law enforcement agencies couldn't. They operated outside the box and under an international umbrella of exemption. Something like diplomatic immunity... on steroids.

When the door-lock clicked open, Logan made his way down the hall to the office of his immediate superior. Chief Carl Platt ran this field office of ETC and his position commanded enough control to order an agent on or off a case. Logan didn't envy him his job, quite sure working with such a diverse group could be tougher than herding chickens in rush hour traffic.

Logan hadn't even sat down when Platt cut straight to the chase.

"Organized?"

"International." Logan handed him a file folder.

Platt leaned forward, his six-foot frame halfway

across the desk. "Your specialty is getting inside organized crime in *North America*."

Logan held his ground. "But I can smell this one."

Platt sat back and crossed his arms. "Fill me in. We'll see if I pick up an odor."

Platt's gaze was steady, and Logan had no doubt his body language, his gestures, and everything else down to heart rate was being noted as he laid out the details. He made sure his passion for the project was unmistakable. And to top off his supervisor's interest, Logan emphasized his suspicion of Eastern Bloc involvement.

Platt shook his head. "Sounds like it belongs to the FBI or Interpol. Why should ETC get involved? Are you getting a connection?"

"I'm working on it. I feel the opening, almost get a read, then she blocks me."

"She knows you're telepathic?"

"I haven't said anything, nor has she, but I'm certain she knows. She forgets sometimes, but then slams the defenses into place before I can slip in."

"There's the question, Logan. Can you play her? Or is she playing you?"

Logan fought back a sigh. "Some of each."

"Okay, your gut says this is big, international, but what's your head saying? Sum it up for me."

"She's trouble. She knows exactly what she's doing and she knows what she wants from me. She's using me."

"And where does that leave you?"

"Just inside the door, not taking off my coat," he said with a grimace.

Platt threw back his head and laughed. "Jesus, Logan, you know how to bump into this kind, don't you?"

Logan held up his hands. "I think they find me."

Platt's face grew serious. "You're not working alone this time. You need someone with objectivity."

"Respectfully, sir, I work best alone."

"So you think. But I'm assigning you an anchor this time."

"But—"

"Logan, I'm feeling this one myself."

"Really?"

Platt stared again at the file photo of Isaac and Grace dancing mere hours before the murder. He didn't tell Logan he'd met her before, didn't mention the sister. "This woman's in trouble and I don't know if we can make a difference." He lifted his gaze to Logan. "Play along. Do what you have to do, but every single piece of information comes back here to me, personally."

"Sir?"

"You've got full run without an anchor, but that's subject to change. You'll have Brad for research and me for back-up." As Logan nodded, Platt held up a hand. "But if I say you're coming out, it won't be negotiable.

#

Thirty-six hours later, Brad left Logan a short message. "Poker. My place. Seven o'clock. Bring pizza."

Logan arrived with a large pepperoni in one hand,

a six-pack in the other, and the hope that Brad had found answers.

"Took you long enough. Did you find something useful?"

"What kind of useful were you looking for, pal?" Brad took the pizza box and led the way to the kitchen table.

Logan popped the tops on a couple of beers and passed one to Brad who was already tucking into the pizza. "Grace doesn't want the investigation into her father's murder reopened. She's tossed a reason or two at me, but they don't ring true. I get the feeling there's something major she's not telling me. Yet I can feel it in my gut that she wants me to push."

Brad's mouth twitched. "One of those yes-no-yes-no kind of women?"

Logan shook his head. "No. More like a half-starved dog snarling at you even though you're offering a big tasty chunk of steak. She's terrified I'll get closer."

Brad nodded and chased the hot cheese and pepperoni with cold beer before reeling off the information he'd uncovered. "I'll start with Isaac. Squeaky clean, model American citizen. Not even a lousy parking ticket. Grown son of Katarina Petrovna, father unknown, graduated high school in Boston and that's where the information stops."

Logan's eyebrows were raised in question, prompting Brad to continue.

"Seems his life after that became very private. So much so, that he was protected under the UIPD— United Intelligence Protection Doctrine—even though no agency claims him as theirs. He traveled extensively with a multitude of different identities. I've accessed those files, but they're coded.

"That's it? You get pizza for nothing more than what I'd already guessed?"

Brad laughed at him. "I get pizza *and beer* because I can get through back doors and into information loops undetected."

Logan grinned. "Spill."

"I've dug up some significant pieces of the puzzle. There's more to unlock but it's taking time. Isaac was born to prima ballerina Katarina Petrovna seven months after she defected to America. He was groomed as a dancer from the day he was born, attended a school for gifted children in Boston, spoke several languages fluently before the age of ten. At fifteen, he was sent to an undisclosed university and by twenty, had earned a doctorate in communication."

Brad reached for another slice of pizza. "While in university he had a short romance with an up-and-coming music sensation known as Meredith, but was dumped when she signed a contract with a European record company and left school mid-semester, relocating to France.

"Upon finishing his degrees, Isaac became a choreographer with his mother's dance company. Years later, while touring in Europe, he was photographed coming out of a hotel with Meredith. The tabloid running the picture which included a gawky ten-year-old, who bore a remarkable resemblance to Isaac, speculated that he was the child's father. Strangely, I found no other documentation about the child, but Meredith did make headlines for the next few weeks as she was spotted several times, sunbathing *au naturel*, in the south of France."

"Distraction tactics," said Logan.

Nodding in agreement, Brad continued. "When Isaac left the dance company, he bought an old property about two hours from here and created a country inn called Paradise. He also owned similar properties in California, Florida, Texas, Hawaii, Anchorage, Alaska and two in Canada. These properties are frequently used by the rich and famous."

"So, why the secrecy?"

"Don't know yet. But chances are, if I keep digging, I'll either find out or someone will pay me a visit."

"What about his daughter?" Logan asked as he popped the top off another beer and passed it to Brad.

"Grace Taylor, born to Meredith Taylor, no father on record. Resided in fourteen different countries and three states before the age of eighteen. No record of ever attending school, did her S.A.T.s at sixteen— nearly perfect scores. At about the age of ten, she was considered to be a gifted dancer. She went into training with a master in France, suffered an injury, and stopped dancing altogether. Attended university in Europe, has a master's degree in," he paused a beat, "communications. Fluent in seven languages. Has never declared employment. All her reported income is from investments."

"Something wrong with that picture."

"I agree. Both bios are missing important pieces."

"Do me a favor and run Meredith for me. I think she—" Logan didn't finish the sentence. "Do Katarina as well. Between the two of them, there may be a clue."

"Sure," Brad answered. "What about telepathy,?"

Logan went to the fridge, helped himself to a soda. "Every time I get a glimpse into her mind, she slams the door shut. I have a feeling she reads as well as I do."

"Oh-ho, that complicates things," Brad said with a grin.

"Makes it damned interesting for sure. So I also need you to dig up anything and everything about Grace's connections, partners, love-life."

"You looking for something specific?"

"Full history. Any and every tidbit you can find."

"Anything else?"

"Yeah, you gonna eat the last piece?"

Chapter 9

Sarah studied Grace as she prowled the room, tapping her fists against the windowsill and rubbing her knuckles together.

"Sit down," Sarah commanded.

Grace tossed her a frustrated look, shook her head, plunked herself in a chair, and huffed out an impatient sigh, her two words as brittle as glass: "I'm edgy."

Sarah laughed. "I feel so enlightened."

"Sorry."

"Why did you call me today, Grace?"

"Because I wanted to call Logan and couldn't."

"So you came here instead? I don't understand." As always, Sarah would have to drag the clues out of her.

Grace tipped her head back and sighed. "I fed him information. If I've sparked his interest, he'll contact me."

"So you baited the hook, and now you're waiting."

"Yeah."

"Ever heard of jigging?"

Her brow furrowed. "No."

"Right now you're doing little more than dangling the bait in the water and hoping the passing fish will see it. Jigging is kind of upping the odds. Subtle jerking of the line causes the bait to jump and wriggle, which improves the odds of the fish spotting it."

Grace shot her a twisted smile. "Where do you get this stuff?"

"I was at my Dad's house once, complaining about how much I hated a couple of my university courses. He sat me down and explained that anything could be interesting if you made the effort to put it into a form you liked. He liked fishing. So he used a bunch of fishing analogies to show me a different way to look at the classes I hated." She grinned. "I know way more about fishing than I should."

"Isaac talked about life in terms of dance. In a casino he'd say things like, 'How about we waltz our way past a couple of tables and see if the music picks up along the way?'"

Sarah was pleased that Grace had spontaneously shared one of her Isaac memories. "You're very lucky to have spent so much time together."

Grace's shoulders stiffened. "Never mind all that. Tell me how to jiggle the bait in front of Logan."

"I don't know, but I think you do."

"I think he has extra abilities," she blurted.

Sarah's eyes widened. "Can you read him?"

"I can feel him. I know there's a door in, but he's got it bolted in a way that makes me think he knows about me."

"About your abilities?"

"I slipped up a couple of times by accident and then once on purpose."

"And that's the bait you're using?"

Grace nodded. "I think we could work together very well."

Sarah laughed. "Must be hard for an honest woman like you to live such a devious double life."

"Glass houses." Grace said with a smirk.

Sarah bit back her response. Took a deep breath and said, "So what do you want from me right now?

"Your help. Tell me how to wiggle the bait to catch the man," she said with a chuckle.

Sarah couldn't help but smile back. Being peeved at Grace just wasn't possible. "Grace, I *do* love you. But sometimes your people skills worry me."

#

Grace tapped on Nancy's office door and was welcomed with a smile.

"Honey, how are you?" she asked as she wrapped her up in a hug.

"Edgy," said Grace drawing away to perch on the brown couch and pull a bright orange pillow into her lap.

Nancy's gaze sharpened. "Not having nightmares again, are you?"

"No. I was afraid they'd start back up, but so far, so good."

"Then what's got you stirred up?"

"Logan."

Nancy turned away to plug in the kettle and take two lime green cups from the shelf. "We'll have tea." She dropped two teabags into a large teapot. "You bother him, too."

Grace's lips twitched. "Really?"

"Oh yeah, really. The question is, what are you going to do about it?"

"Not sure yet. I left the ball in his court."

"But you dropped in to see me just in case he was around so you could bump into him."

"That's so high school Nancy. I came to see you."

"Why?"

"To ask you about the Brontosaurus." Grace grinned.

Nancy laughed. "Divorced, no kids, likes animals, damn good at his job, on loan to us from some fancy federal bureau or agency, staying in a hotel downtown."

"So he's what, FBI? CIA?"

"Not sure, something to do with organized crime. He's got an uncanny ability to find the links. Some say he reads minds. I heard he could sit in a room full of people and pick out the bad guys, tell you who was connected to whom, and he rarely misses."

Grace rubbed the back of her neck to ease the tingling. "So what was he doing here?"

"Part of a task force. That bust you were almost in the middle of? He was the info man on it. Our department could only get halfway to the head guy, the leader, no matter what angle they played. Logan was here for less than two weeks and managed to ferret him out."

"So why's he so interested in Isaac's murder?"

"I think it's you he's interested in."

Grace took a minute to digest that tidbit. It wasn't like she didn't know there was some kind of attraction happening, but something about hearing it out loud sat oddly. "Nan..."

"What, honey?"

"Nothing. I'd better get going. Lots to do today."

"Honey, the kettle's already boiled. Stay and have tea with me."

#

He hadn't heard a sound, but with a shimmering of preternatural awareness, Logan's full attention swung from the file on the table in front of him to the far end of the conference room.

A small dapper-looking fellow stood in the doorway—steel gray hair, gray mustache, dark suit. Shiny black shoes matched his beady eyes. When he stepped into the room and closed the door behind him, Logan rose and pushed back his chair, but made a conscious decision to not reach for his weapon.

"Detective Logan?"

He nodded. "And you are?"

"Dr. Kusavinski, Grace Taylor's psychiatrist."

Logan kept his expression blank. "What can I do for you?"

"Stop the investigation. Miss Taylor's distressing memories have resurfaced due to the incident several days ago, and because her emotional stress manifests as physical pain, I predict her capacity for endurance will be severely limited."

"I'm sorry to hear she's unwell."

"You must stop this nonsense before she experiences another breakdown."

"Breakdown?"

"I have concern regarding her ability to recover if

she requires hospitalization again."

"I see."

"So the investigation will be terminated." The doctor made his question a statement.

"I'll inform my superiors of a problem, and hopefully they'll oblige. I like Grace, and I'd hate to think I was causing her any kind of pain."

"Thank you. I was quite certain you would acquiesce when presented with adequate explanation," said the doctor with a barely perceptible nod. He about-faced with military crispness, let himself out, and closed the door with a distinctive click.

Logan shook his head, opened his laptop, and noted every detail he could recall about the man. He called the security department and they confirmed that Dr. Kusavinski had left the building. They made copies of all digital security data and forwarded copies to his computer.

With hardcopies tucked neatly into his briefcase, Logan grabbed his jacket off the back of a chair and headed for the stairs.

He stopped dead a couple of steps past Nancy's closed door, backed up slowly, then smiled. She was in there.

He pulled out his phone and hit speed dial.

"Nancy, here."

"I need twenty minutes alone with your visitor," he said.

"Really?"

"Come on Nance, be a sport. It's important."

"Well I suppose. Give me a minute, okay?"

He needed the element of surprise. "I'm coming in and I'd rather not have to throw you out."

"Well, if you put it that way, of course I understand. Be right with you."

Grace had no doubt what was going on as she'd felt Logan's presence and made sure he knew she was there when he walked by. And Nancy's body language was ridiculously easy to read, even though her mind wasn't, so Grace was certain her plan had worked.

She smiled when Nancy hung up the phone saying, "Honey, I have to pop out for just a minute. Don't take off on me, okay?"

"No problem." Grace smiled. "Take your time."

When Logan walked in, Grace grinned. *Gottcha.*

"Very nice," he said softly.

She blinked innocently. "Pardon?"

"Still playing games, Grace?"

"Life's one big game, isn't it, Detective?"

Logan loved a challenge. He crossed his arms and leaned against the desk to study her face for a minute. A dare sparkled in her eyes yet her mouth was soft and inviting. "There are games, Grace, and then there are games…"

He opened his mind and projected his thoughts. Imagined leaning toward her, gently rubbing his lips across hers, slipping his tongue across the softness, tasting. She lifted a hand to her mouth and he stifled a grin before going on. Now it was his hands. He imagined them pushing her hair back, his thumbs lifting her jaw, his fingertips feathering over the sensitive skin of her throat then sliding down to the row of buttons between her breasts.

Grace's eyes darkened. A breath caught in her throat and when she clutched the front of her shirt, he grinned, saying softly, "Gotcha back."

Grace kept her expression neutral while she used concentrated breathing to slow her heart rate. "You're good," she said. "And you play dirty."

"You don't?"

"Never said that."

"Didn't have to."

"Would you please sit down? I'm getting a crick in my neck."

Logan sat at the other end of the couch.

"Scared of me, Brontosaurus?"

"No." *Of myself.*

Her eyebrows raised. *Makes two of us.*

"I had a visitor a little while ago. Man claimed to be your shrink. Care to enlighten me?"

Logan watched her close down, just as he'd expected.

"Who was he?" Somehow her voice sounded curious and angry at the same time.

"Same question back at you."

"You saw him, I didn't."

"Dr. Kusavinski. Small man, gray hair, beady eyes."

Grace's stomach lurched and the door to her mind slammed shut. "Assigned to me by the family after Isaac was murdered. Kept me drugged for a while."

"How bad? How long?"

"Out cold for around twenty-four hours, then in a stupor for a few days." She laughed. "First time in my life Meredith's selfishness actually helped me. She didn't want the press to get wind of my mental state. Checked me out of the hospital, hid me away until the drugs wore off. Wouldn't let anyone near me for almost a week." The lies came easily now.

"Do you have flashbacks? Post-Traumatic Stress?"

"Nothing at all."

"Memory loss. How far back Grace?" His voice was soft.

With little effort unshed tears glistened. "Years." She choked back a sob. "I don't remember dancing with him. I only have the pictures as proof. I have no recall of the casinos, the clubs, the beaches, the long lazy afternoons."

Logan took a step toward her, stopped, wanted to shout the single word, *bullshit,* but instead asked a reasonable question. "Is it just your time with Isaac that's gone, or is it your whole life?"

"Just Isaac is gone. Dr. Kusavinski said it was my way of blocking-out the murder."

All too convenient, he thought, and she'd begun to contradict herself. Had to be on purpose though, as she was far too bright for it to be accidental.

"Is that why you don't want the case reopened?" he asked.

Grace laid her cheek against the soft leather, closed her eyes and waited until she could feel him at the doorway of her mind, waiting. She took a deep cleansing breath, carefully formulated her thoughts and let them slip past the barrier. *I'm afraid I'm being manipulated. Imprisoned without walls. Watched and controlled. My life is in danger.*

He reached for her hand, to strengthen the connection and watched her face while he answered in thought, *Why me?*

Because you can hear me.

Others can hear you.

No, they can't.

He allowed her to lead him. *Who else knows about your gift?*

Sarah does.

Did Isaac know?

She squeezed her eyes shut. *I can't remember.*

A sharp pain shot from the base of his skull, encompassed his entire head in a vice-like grip. Pure reflex had him shutting down the telepathic connection between them. The pain vanished, leaving little more than an echo. Sweat dampened the back of his neck.

He focused on her face and was surprised to find it expressionless. "Grace, open your eyes." She did so slowly, and he still saw no sign of the pain he'd just experienced.

"You don't believe I can't remember," she said.

"Do you have a headache?"

She frowned. "Not yet but I'll get one if I try to search for memories."

"Don't try."

Grace was surprised by the sharpness of his voice. She studied him, waited to hear his thoughts but instead felt the strength of his resistance. "What's wrong?"

"You're about to have a blinding headache."

"How do you know?"

"I can feel it. Let's get you out of here."

Chapter 10

A blinding headache? Much to her own surprise, Grace accepted—without question or concern—the logic of Logan's statement. His hotel was closer than her place, therefore, that was where they'd go. She glanced at him when she got into his car. Was it just the telepathy or had he used other powers to make her feel this comfortable with him?

He said nothing as they pulled into traffic and she continued to ponder. He'd showed no annoyance when she'd shut down their telepathic link. Made no attempt to shove past her block. Yes, he'd blatantly manipulated the situation, but she had to respect his honesty. Because when it came to manipulation... She stopped herself and refused to go any further with that pointless train of thought.

Observing the man now, she noted that although he monitored the mirror and constantly flexed his fingers on the steering wheel, she felt no apprehension. In fact, she was reminded of riding shotgun with Isaac. The warmth that came with that thought was immediately followed by a flash of fire radiating from the back of her neck. Recognizing the warning, she swallowed hard and threw herself into the present with gusto.

She concentrated on looking afraid—raised her eyebrows and went for a wide-eyed look while she clenched her fists in her lap. Making her voice sound breathless, she said, "Do you think we're being followed? Is that why you're watching the mirrors that way?"

He swung his gaze to study her and shook his head. "No. Sorry. Just a reflex. Call it a byproduct of the job." Returning his focus to the road in front of them, he asked, "Why aren't you concerned about the killer headache I've predicted?"

She shrugged. "Pain's a part of my life. I've learned to live with it."

"You normally medicate. Why don't you keep the meds with you?"

"Not much point when I can't drive once I take them." Which wasn't exactly true. "Besides you've promised to fix me up with some magic instead. And color me weird, but I believe you."

Logan's uneasiness increased. And with it came the leading edge of fear. For her. *Of* her. Something very complicated swirled around this woman, never fully visible yet never completely gone. His frustration had grown with the recognition of both honesty and deceit mingled with fear and detachment. But there was something more, as though he was being set up. But his instincts weren't warning him away from her. To the contrary, he couldn't seem to stay away—and that confused the hell out of him.

"Almost there, so we'll get to the magic real soon. Meantime, anything else you'd like to tell me about? Anything at all?"

"No, why?"

He angled the car into a parking spot on the street about a half block away from his hotel.

"You could have parked in the underground. I wouldn't have freaked out."

"Your headache doesn't need any more triggers right now, not when it's about to light up."

"Light up," she murmured. "What a perfect description. I can feel it starting now."

Grace could no longer ignore the fire at the back of her neck as it morphed into pressure and pain moving upward with sinister intent, spreading out, flexing cruel fingers into her skull.

Next, she could expect to feel as if her brain was swelling, becoming too big, pushing and fighting for escape. The final stage was the one she hated the most. The unbearably brilliant, blazing light behind her eyes that meant the headache was fully engaged and there was nothing left to do but ride it out. Preferably while asleep, thereby avoiding the explosions of pain and the nausea that came with them.

Thinking about the symptoms had been a mistake, as though opening the door to reality. And by the time they reached his room, the pressure in her head was becoming unbearable.

When Logan pulled heavy drapes across the window and pointed at the bed, she surprised herself— and probably him—by stripping down to her pale blue teddy and crawling under the covers, curling into herself. When he sat on the edge beside her, she opened one eye and watched him set a glass of water on the night stand. *Those beautiful hands again. Touch me.*

"Close your eyes and turn onto your stomach."

His hands settled between her shoulder blades, worked outward, pushing and prodding at knotted muscles. Grace was silent as each area loosened and he moved on to the next. But when he pushed her hair aside to touch her neck she shifted and began to mumble.

Logan hesitated, leaned down to hear her, and noted an odd tingling that began where his hands rested on her neck and moved up his arms.

"My head, now. Please," she begged.

"It'll be better if I loosen your neck first." He stroked the hair back from her temples.

She swallowed and with more emphasis said, "Leave my neck. Please, my head now."

Conceding in silence, he adjusted her head on the pillow and began with a feather-light touch over her temples, worked under to her brows and below her eyes. Sweeping around and around with increasing pressure until he was working the tension away, forcing each muscle to release. Using his thumbs, he pressed hard, applying steady pressure to trigger points around her ears, and was rewarded by her long deep exhale indicating she'd fallen asleep. Glancing at the clock, he noted it'd taken nearly an hour to give her relief from the pain.

He stood and stretched, walked to the window, and pushed the drapes aside to look out. Her sharply drawn breath had him cursing softly, and he let the curtain fall back across the light.

"I'm sorry. I thought you were sleeping."

"Not quite."

"Is it getting worse?"

She hesitated just long enough for him to know.

He went to the bottom of the bed, pulled out the covers and folded them back to expose her feet.

"What the hell are you doing?" she muttered.

"Trying to get rid of your headache."

"I need my meds."

"What do you take?"

"Pain blockers, sedatives, the usual."

He could feel the evasiveness. "You take anything over the counter?"

She half-laughed, then winced. "Tried it all, nothing helps."

He went to the bathroom, came back, and told her to sit up. He dropped half a white pill in her hand and passed her the water glass.

"What is it?"

"Do you care?"

Grace shrugged, popped it into her mouth, and chased it with half a glass of water. The blood in her brain was doing that ugly double-thump now, like oil in a lava lamp, slopping in slow motion from back to front inside her skull. She looked up at him and the thumping increased its pace, making her cringe.

"Put your head back down."

She settled on the pillow, held her breath for as long as she could, then finally let it out with a moan. "Jesus. Talk to me Logan. Do something to distract me until the drugs work."

He smiled wickedly. "Oh how I'd like to distract you, Princess."

"Anything," she challenged in a whisper. "Please Logan."

His lips gently teased, feathering kisses over her forehead, her eyelids, across her cheekbones, and then her mouth. She sighed softly and he eased away, turned his back to her, and took one of her feet between his hands.

When she flinched, he said, "I promise it will help, Grace. Just relax." And he was right. This was no gentle massage. He forcefully worked the tension out of her feet, paying close attention to the pressure points and meridians. Her baby toes had never had such attention. His knuckles pushed deep into the arch and spread her toes to open the channels and allow relief to flow.

Logan watched her face in the dim light and saw the tension begin to ebb. He continued to work her feet for nearly an hour before sliding his hand to the back of her knee. She never moved and he smiled. This time she was definitely asleep.

He eased up from the bed and rolled his cramped shoulders. He contemplated the two chairs, then the small sofa, shrugged, undressed, pulled on sweats and a t-shirt. He stretched out on top of the covers beside her, turned on his side to watch her sleep, and listened to her even breathing while he wondered.

#

She woke up feeling safe and oddly comfortable. Oddly because, even though she had no idea where she was, no fear trickled in. The room was very dark but she knew she was in a hotel by the smell of the sheets. She moved with care, slowly settled onto her back to check out her surroundings, and realization crept in.

It was Logan's warmth beside her, not Milo's. How she'd come to be there slipped through her mind as she stared at the back of his head, wondering what would happen between them now. She longed to touch him, but caution held her back.

She remembered the feel of his lips on her face, his hands on her sensitive feet, and she grew warm wondering what would happen if she just reached out her hand and—

His voice was soft, husky. "Careful Grace. I can hear you." He rolled over slowly and smiled at her. "And I'm just as curious as you are so feel free."

She didn't move. "I'm thinking this isn't the time for boldness."

"You lie, Grace. That's not what you're thinking." His fingers slid down her arm.

"Why do you want light?" she asked.

"Oh nicely done. Do you want an answer or do you already know?"

"You blocked too quickly." And she didn't want him gaining access to her mind right now. "Tell me the answer out loud."

"I would like to watch you. See what goes on in those feline eyes when I touch you."

"Wouldn't you rather read my thoughts to know what I'm feeling?"

"You can block me and have control over everything but the changing color of your eyes. They don't lie."

Mentally she drew back, and he chuckled softly. "See?"

She went for a safer subject. "What was that pill you gave me, Detective?"

"Just a little something to take you past the pain."

"Nothing more?"

Logan could see and feel the wariness in her. "Scout's honor," he promised. "Hungry?"

"Not really. What time is it?"

Logan pushed the button on the side of his watch and the face glowed pale blue. "Six fifteen." He caught her frantic thought and grabbed her just in time. "Careful. Move slowly or take a chance with the head."

"I need to get home." She eased herself up.

"I'll take you."

"I can drive myself." She sat on the side of the bed, staring at her clothes on the floor as though wondering if she dared to bend over to get them.

"Don't." Logan circled the bed, passed her the clothes, and then walked into the bathroom without a backward glance.

Grace's mind began to wander and she brought herself up short. How the hell much could Logan read? Was she able to have a single private thought? Could he read through the closed door?

Chapter 11

Logan emerged from the bathroom, black jeans molding long muscular thighs. A royal blue polo shirt accentuated his broad shoulders and highlighted the color of his eyes.

The sizzle and punch of chemistry warmed Grace from the inside out.

"Why, thank you," he said with a grin that was gone so fast she wondered if she'd imagined it. "As you suspected, Grace, I'm picking up your thoughts quite easily now. And while I don't mind knowing how you feel about my wardrobe, I think you could use some pointers on how to block your thoughts more effectively."

"Can't handle a compliment?"

"I don't want to be accused of lurking in your mind or spying on your thoughts. Why don't we order some dinner and talk for a while?"

"Works for me. I don't remember when I ate last." She glanced at the room service menu Logan handed her. "To be clear though, I'm not looking forward to being questioned, but I know it's part of the drill."

"Ground rules first, then. The next hour is about

food, techniques to help you selectively block your thoughts, and protection of your internal voice."

It sounded good in theory, but there would be more, and it would take more than an hour. She glanced at her watch. Milo and Careless would be okay as long as she was home by midnight.

With a twinkle in his eye, he said, "They'll be fine."

She frowned. "Stop eavesdropping."

"Stop broadcasting."

"Teach me," she said, careful to have her thoughts mirror her words.

His sharp look made her wonder if he could tell she was trying to deceive him. She smiled. "I'll have the shrimp sandwich, toasted, on white, with coleslaw. And a bottle of water, please."

He ordered himself a steak sandwich with fries, gravy, and coffee.

When she raised an eyebrow and thought, *dessert*, he added apple pie and triple chocolate cake to the list. She chuckled. "Two desserts?"

"Couldn't decide which one you'd like," he answered with a smile. "Now, let's get started."

In the forty minutes it took for their meal to arrive, he walked her through a series of visualization techniques for completely and partially blocking her thoughts from intruders.

In spite of being adept at other methods she'd either invented or had stumbled upon, she listened carefully and experimented as he instructed. Having more tricks up her sleeve was never a bad thing. But she was glad when the food was delivered.

Silence settled comfortably between them as they

ate until Grace finished the pie, moved on to the cake, and became acutely aware of his surreptitious study.

"Metabolism," she said.

The crease between his eyebrows deepened.

"What's wrong?" she asked.

"You shouldn't have been able to hear that."

Now she grinned at him. "I didn't. Your astonishment at the amount of food I was eating was written all over your face. You must be used to women who live on lettuce." She licked the last bit of chocolate icing off her fork. "I love food, and lucky for me, my metabolism allows me to eat what I want."

"How old were you when you discovered your extra abilities?"

All humor left her expression. "Talk about an abrupt change of subject." She reached for her water, took a long swallow, then settled back in her chair.

"There was no moment of discovery. I don't remember a time when I *didn't* hear thoughts not my own. Apparently I was born this way. And I was very, very, young when I realized I was different than other people. Being a bright child, it didn't take long for me to learn to keep what I heard to myself."

"Did that make you sad?"

"Not overly, but I did become inwardly focused for a while. My own weird mix of telepathy and mind-reading became my world in a way."

"In what way?" he prodded.

"Long story. I'll give you the condensed version." She pushed away from the small table and sat cross-legged on one of the loveseats. "I was born in France, where Meredith's career had taken off in the months leading up to my birth."

"You're a French citizen?"

"No." She held up her hands. "A different story for another day. Anyhow, my mother's career sailed on brilliantly in Europe after I was born. Music, videos, movies."

She gave him a twisted smile. "Being hailed as a marvelous mother, she took me everywhere she went. Posed for photos, showed off the child she'd been willing to—" she used her fingers for air quotes, "—keep even if it meant a sacrifice to her career." She shook her head. "In reality, I was mostly squirreled away into corners of sound stages, and silence was the first rule I learned."

When she hesitated, Logan said nothing.

Grace leaned her head back and closed her eyes. "I wasn't allowed to speak, make any kind of noise, couldn't even look at a book or color because the sensitive equipment would pick up the sound of pages turning. And, in spite of my name, I was a clumsy child, so I guess there was fear I'd drop a crayon or something. I spent hours on end, watching, absorbing, and listening to the often conflicting thoughts and actions of dozens of people."

"Bet you felt like your head would pop."

"Yeah. And when I tried to block it out or concentrate too hard, it hurt."

"How'd you deal with headaches when you were so young?"

She opened her eyes and met his gaze head on. "If a whimper or two escaped me, something would be popped into my juice, or a little smoke would be blown in my face, whatever it took to protect the silence."

"Fucking criminal treatment." Logan said through gritted teeth.

Grace shrugged. "Not exactly a perfect childhood, but nobody beat me, I didn't go hungry, and I had a clean, warm, hotel bed to sleep in every night. Eventually, she started to leave me in the room when she went to a shoot."

"Alone?"

"No, I'll give her credit for trying, she always hired a babysitter."

"How did that work out?"

"She called them tutors." Grace's half laugh was without humor. "They may have even been certified, but we were in Europe until I was twelve. My lessons, the books from the States were in English, and my tutors were always locals who didn't speak English."

"Child Protection Services should have been called. Somebody should have hung her by her thumbs for neglect."

"Actually, it turned out okay, because I developed an ear for languages."

"That was your childhood?" he growled. "Holed up in hotels with strangers? Learning foreign languages?"

She straightened with a frown. "Of course not." She went to the window and stared out over the city. "My childhood may not have been spent playing with dolls, rollicking on playgrounds, and learning silly games, but it *was* filled with diverse and beneficial experiences that prepared me for an independent life. I was blessed with the kind of grooming that produces social maturity and self-reliance."

"Sounds like a sales pitch your mother would have made."

She spun to face him, waving her hands as she spoke. "Before I was eight, I could order a five-course meal in a fancy restaurant, choose the appropriate wine, and use the correct fork. I helped Meredith select wardrobe, men, lyrics, and even backup dancers."

Logan felt her flinch in the single heartbeat between words.

"As I grew older, I assisted on-set and behind the camera. I rehearsed scenes and read lines with her. My life was filled to the brim and pretty darned exciting."

"Did the headaches go away?"

She drew in a long breath, let it out slowly. "Not altogether, but they were less frequent once I'd taught myself how to filter."

"Were you able to stop using drugs to manage the pain?"

"I utilized a variety of tools to hold off the flood of unwanted information, to block out what I didn't want to hear."

Logan dropped his voice an octave in an attempt to hide the censure stirred up by her carefully worded reply. "Do you still need medications?"

"As you're aware from your visit to my home, I use prescriptions for psychologically-induced migraine headaches."

As far as he knew, a psychologist wouldn't be licensed to prescribe pharmaceuticals, so that left Sarah out. "Prescribed by your MD or Dr. Kusavinski?"

"Kusavinski." She went back to the loveseat, curled herself into the corner as though making herself as small as she could.

He softened his voice again. "Why don't you tell

me about how he came to be your psychiatrist?"

She closed her eyes.

"Grace." He waited until she looked at him. "Do you trust me?"

"I have to, you can read my mind."

He leaned forward, braced his elbows on his knees, and loosely linked his hands together. "I can't help you if you don't trust me."

"I said I do."

"And you're lying."

Grace stared at him, her eyes searching his, looking for something she hoped she'd recognize. "You make me uncomfortable. Why are we here, Logan? Why the interest?"

"I got some kind of a cosmic jolt of connection the moment I laid eyes on you, and I don't believe in coincidence."

"What the hell does that mean?" she asked, although not certain she was ready for his answer.

"Being completely plugged into the bust, the timing, the adrenaline, when I felt the connection, I misinterpreted the message. My visceral response was overlaid with both annoyance that you were in the way, and my purely male reaction to your appearance."

Her eyebrows went up and she whispered, "Drop-dead-fucking-gorgeous-woman."

He grimaced. "You heard me. That's why you stopped and looked around."

"Yeah, scared hell out of me, didn't know where it was coming from. Got rid of the shoes so I could run." She hesitated. "Go on."

"After the bust, dragging you out from under the

car and handing you over to Nancy, I felt something again, but chalked it up to either my adrenaline hangover, my annoyance with your attitude, or my own guilt."

"Guilt?"

"I knew I'd scared the daylights out of you and I felt bad."

"Now who's lying?"

"Okay, I felt bad because I didn't feel the least bit remorseful."

"That's better. Now tell me why the interest developed."

"The next morning, when I saw your pain, the headache, I could almost feel it. I've had a few of my own. It's the price one pays for the extra-sensory package."

"Okay, that explains why you dropped the verbal sparring and sent me off to bed so quickly. Why you knew to shut out the light, bring me water."

He smiled. "I heard you then and realized why I was there."

"What did you hear?"

Logan studied her face, knew he could tell her part of the truth, wasn't sure about the rest. Didn't want to scare her, but, dammit, he wanted to scare her.

He closed the distance between them, perched on the edge of the seat, and reached for her hand. He ran his fingertips along the scar that stretched from palm to elbow, a fine ridge in the soft flesh.

Grace's heart jerked. She could feel the question in his mind and fought to keep the answer from him, from herself. She wanted to pull away from his touch, his power, yet wanted to fall into it, too. Drown in him. She began to shake and his direct gaze didn't leave hers.

"You asked me to touch you." His smile was wry. "It amused me that I could hear your thoughts. I was thinking purely as a man looking at a beautiful woman who wanted my hands on her. For an instant, I was annoyed Nancy was in the kitchen, because I wanted to climb into bed with you."

Her heart bumped. "Opportunist," she muttered but didn't pull her hand away.

He shook his head. "When I finally did let myself touch you, I took it right between the eyes. Your mind latched onto mine while you were drifting away. Your subconscious screamed at me to help you. You were clawing and scraping past the drugs, determined not to let them take you away, begging me to help you."

"You just tapped into a bad dream I was having. I'm fine. I don't need you." She jumped up and tried to turn away, but his grip tightened on her hand.

Now face-to-face, he grabbed her chin and forced her to meet his eyes. "That's where you're wrong, lady. You do need me."

"I don't *want* to go back. Just let it go, Logan. Leave me alone."

"To live your life through drugs and denial, Grace? Is that what you want? Or was the voice I heard that night the real you? The truth you're afraid to acknowledge."

She changed tactics, moved into him, pressed her body against his, and tried to ignore the brilliant flash of awareness. Putting huskiness in her voice took no effort. "Why not just leave my messed-up mind alone and have a bit of fun?" She slid her arms around his neck and stroked her lips across his, tasting, teasing.

His hands fisted in her hair and he dragged her mouth away from his. "I don't like games," he said, then sunk into her. Kissed her long, slow, and deep, his power driving straight to the center of her being. His tongue explored. Her bones liquefied. And there wasn't a thought left in her head when he drew his mouth from hers. "And this, is not what we came here for."

"What?" Her voice shook.

"I plan to tie myself to you for the next few weeks, Grace, but it's not about sex."

"Too bad," she murmured. "We'd be good."

A smile threatened at the corners of his mouth while something complicated lurked in his eyes. "No doubt there, but it's not the reason we met." Fingertips teased the edge of her mouth, trailed down to the pulse in her throat and the lurking smile bloomed, spreading across his face. "Even if you are drop-dead-fucking-gorgeous." He planted one last firm kiss on her stunned mouth. "Get your shoes; I'm taking you home."

Chapter 12

Logan couldn't help but grin at the dog's antics when Grace let him in through the sliding glass door. A blur of black, he sailed from room to room, zipping over and under furniture, out of control like a balloon with the end untied.

"Where did you get this silly creature?" he asked as the absurdity slowed to full-body wriggling.

"Stray," she replied as though distracted.

He watched as she stepped outside and methodically scanned the circumference of the pool area. Shoulders visibly relaxing, she came back in, dimmed the outdoor lighting, and reset security. When Milo bumped against her legs, she leaned down and absently rubbed his head.

"Pound puppies make such great pets," he said, trying to draw her back from wherever she'd gone.

She frowned. "He wasn't a puppy when I got him. He had issues, needed a home, and we hit it off."

He studied her face, contemplated slipping into her mind, but that would only serve to strip away the tentative foundation of trust.

"He's a good match for you. Happy. Grateful." He chuckled when the big white cat rubbed against the dog's chest. "And he likes cats."

"Please don't tell me you can read animals."

He laughed. "Hell, no. But he's fun to watch."

"Once your eyes adjust to how homely he is," she said with a smile for the dog whose tongue lolled out as they studied him.

Logan studied Milo with mock seriousness. "*Unique* is a better word for the physical attributes from his mixed heritage." He tipped his head like a dog. "Border Collie, Lab, Shepherd, and maybe some Rottie in that wide smile."

She nodded. "That hits the outside to a tee, but as for his weird mind, and hating all cats but Careless…" She shrugged. "Who knows? That's probably more do to with his life before we met."

"Careless? That's your cat's name?"

"I went through three cats, on a trial basis of course, before I found one that could care less about Milo. Plays with him when the mood strikes, ignores him when it suits, frequently stares at him as if he's calling Milo rude names. They're a perfect match." She smiled. "And he *is* careless, always knocking something off a shelf or table."

"Is that why your home has so little on display? No knickknacks, pictures, plants, and stuff?"

She shrugged. "I'm away a lot and was never into that kind of thing anyway."

Not one to pussyfoot around, he said, "I'd like a tour."

"Curiosity or sweeping for devices?"

"Both." He watched her for reaction and caught the strained look before she turned away. "Help yourself," she said with a flick of her hand. "You don't need a guide."

"Actually, it would be better if you were with me."

Grace fought the automatic wave of distrust and tried to temper her response. "So you can try to pick up handy tidbits from my head?"

"No, because I'd feel less like an intruder in your home."

She allowed the snarl to surface. "I call bullshit." Her jaw clenched and her nostrils widened. "You're a cop, Logan. You had no problem searching my room at Paradise."

"I'm not a cop. Anymore."

"What the hell does that mean?" she snapped.

"I'm a special investigator. I do research, profiling, and undercover work for agencies like the FBI, CIA, CISIS, and Interpol."

Interpol. Isaac. Pain shot through her. Fire burned up her spine, ricocheted inside her head, then icy cold rained down and outward.

She turned her back on him. "You want tea?" Her voice vibrated in her throat, and sounded *off*.

She grew clumsier as she lost motor-control. Her back was to him when the spoon clattered to the counter. Her shaking hands tried to grip the edge, she leaned forward, willing herself to breathe as she begged her heart to slow. Numbness started at her fingertips, rapidly fanned upward, and a groan escaped her throat as she crumpled to the floor.

Logan dove, barely saving her head from smashing on the slate. He slipped his fingers to the base of her throat and found her pulse strangely hard and fast. He frowned.

"Grace?" he tried out loud first, then telepathically, *Grace?* He concentrated, listening for her response. Nothing but total blackness where he used to feel fire as she tried to keep her thoughts from him.

By the time he got her off the floor, onto her bed, and covered with a blanket, his confusion had deepened. Her heart still raced, her breathing was shallow, her skin remained ice cold but not clammy, and her mind was inaccessible.

He left her there and went to the bathroom, opened the medicine cabinet and found more than a dozen pill bottles. He quickly scanned the labels—muscle relaxers, sedatives, pain killers, no narcotics. Nothing he recognized that she could be addicted to, dependent on. But several containers were unlabeled. He took one pill from each of those, wrapped them in a tissue, and dropped them into his pocket.

When he returned to her, panic grabbed him by the throat. Her eyes were open, glazed over, dull, like in death. He groped for the pulse in her neck. It still raced but had weakened to a flutter. He called her name, tapped her cheeks, rubbed his knuckles roughly over her breastbone. Nothing. Totally unresponsive.

Logan noticed the half-opened drawer of her nightstand and cursed when he spotted a tiny plastic container half-filled with pink pills. The lid was gone. He found it in her clenched hand. He gripped her jaw, felt the tightness, pried her mouth open, and cursed at the sight of what he'd hoped not to see, the remains of several pills, pink, almost completely dissolved on her tongue. Without thought his finger swept in, removed what he could.

"Fucking hell," he growled.

And from Grace's mind came the faintest echo, *Fucking hell*.

Moments later, he raced down the stairs with her limp body draped over his shoulder, glad he'd put his car in her garage. There would be no witnesses. He laid her across the front seat so her head would be in his lap while he drove, and backed out quickly, pointing the car north.

Trusting his gut, he opted to bypass the local hospital, head for one of the finest medical facilities in the country, and request help to get her there alive. He used the on-board satellite phone to call for resources.

He kept a hand on Grace's throat to monitor her thready pulse, and twice pulled to the curb to pick up lone figures waiting for him. Each brought jump kits and specialized equipment with them.

The advanced life support paramedics worked quietly together, reaching over the back of the seat to administer oxygen, run leads to a heart monitor, attach a plastic clip to her finger, and establish an IV line in the back of her hand.

After a few minutes, one of the medics touched his shoulder and said, "She's holding her own."

Logan had been on enough assignments with these guys to know his questions wouldn't be welcome, so he didn't ask. For the moment, her life was in their hands.

He made one last call.

"Nancy, its Logan. Grace and I left her place in a hurry. Would you mind going over and making sure the security is set and the pets are okay?"

"What happened?"

"Long story. I'll be in touch."

"Blessed good thing I trust you."

"Thanks."

Chapter 13

Logan's jaw clenched and his stomach muscles tightened as he waited at Grace's bedside. The doctor stood on the opposite side while a nurse positioned at the head of the bed slipped a needle into the IV port and pushed medication with a slow steady hand.

For the third time in as many hours, Grace's eyes opened but didn't focus. The doctor leaned over and spoke to her, flicked the tiny flashlight toward her eyes, touched her face, rubbed her cheek ever so slightly and then the horror began again.

Her eyes cleared. Her body went stiff. She threw out her arms as though fending off an invisible assailant. And she screamed, over and over again, "Isaaaac! Help me! Isaaaac!"

The doctor laid a comforting hand on her shoulder, and just like the last two times they'd forced her awake, she lashed out, viciously swinging her arms and kicking the blankets off her legs. Her screams morphed into the horrible guttural sounds of someone being tortured.

Having seen this twice already, the medical team had a sedative ready, and within seconds of it reaching her vein, Grace's movements slowed, her arms appeared rubbery, she looked drunk, and the sounds she made became whimpers until she went limp and slid into oblivion. Disappeared.

Logan sat with her for ten minutes before wandering out to talk to the team about how to deal with her unusual condition.

It had been three days since he'd brought her in and the blood work had come back the same, over and over again. The vast number of unidentified chemicals in her system weren't wearing off. There had to be an internal source. Something very sophisticated that couldn't be identified using basic scans.

The decision was made.

Grace would be moved from this very special private hospital to another facility—a place with even more sophisticated machinery and a diverse internationally-respected team of experts. A place where traditional medicine merged with every other medical, scientific, psychic, and metaphysical discipline known to man. A place where miracles happened.

In the empty hours between midnight and dawn, when truck drivers felt in command of the world, loading, unloading, looking after business, Grace's stretcher was wheeled into a nondescript transport van and taken to a place of great secrecy. A place hidden beneath the gently rolling hills and manicured greens of an elite golf course on the outskirts of the state capital. Fountains, drains, and clusters of trees cleverly hid the movement of air, the workings of an underground, completely self-contained city. The heart and home of Etcetera.

#

Two hours after her journey, with preliminary testing complete, Grace was wheeled through a door labeled, *Diagnostic Scanning*, and left alone in the center of a room filled with ominous-looking machinery.

Separated from the ETC Advanced Experimental Medical team by a wall of safety glass, draped in a white sheet that glowed under a muted spotlight while the rest of the room was in shadow, she looked lifeless, like an offering on an altar.

Logan was given a seat at the back of the room where the team was gathered, beyond the banks of monitors manned by doctors and researchers who reviewed data as it came to them.

Instead, he stood near the window of the darkened room, watching the huge machines slide into place and scan Grace's body for heat sources, chemical intensities, radioactivity, and foreign objects.

Logan felt responsible. Somehow, he'd slipped into a role of guardian as the days had passed after her collapse. And while those days had been long, the nights were much longer. In his gut, he was afraid Grace had been drugged to the point of no return. He'd tried repeatedly to look into her mind and found nothing but a chilling, black, empty space.

"Hallelujah," sighed a tech at the third desk over.

"What? What did you find?" Logan strode to his side, looked over his shoulder at a screen where a mass of bright colors blended into the shape of a person.

"Implanted chemical concentrations," the tech said. "Holy shit, what a number they did on her. Look at these." He pointed to a scattering of purple spots at the base of her neck. "Jesus she's full of shit. Who the hell's behind all this? Who is she?"

Logan muttered, "Innocent victim. Wrong place, wrong time. Doesn't even know what hit her."

He hoped to hell he wasn't wrong.

#

The microscopic implants were removed and she was allowed to wake up slowly.

This time, when her eyes opened yet didn't focus, it was Logan who leaned over. He kept his voice low and soft. "Grace? Wake up for me, Grace."

She blinked.

The dull gold of her eyes brightened ever so slightly. She tried to speak, but her voice croaked. Logan put a straw to her lips and she took a tiny swallow of cool water, wincing as it woke up her days' dry throat, then tried again. "Logan? Where am I?"

Dr. Kelton leaned into view from the other side of the bed and smiled at her. "Welcome back, Grace."

Like a switch had been thrown, her face changed and terrified, blood-curdling screams cut through the air as she lurched toward him, her fingers curling into claws aimed at his face. The poor doctor jumped back while Logan grabbed her arms and held her against the pillows. "Grace." He shook her ever so slightly. "Grace, it's okay."

She instantly went limp and stared into his eyes. "Logan," she whispered. "Please, Logan." She started to tremble and a sob escaped. "Please, Isaac, don't let him. Please, Isaac," she begged as her knees came up and she rolled onto her side, curling into herself. "No, please no. Please don't touch me." And then she lay still, looking physically frozen, her arms wrapped around her knees, singing softly in French, a child's song so well known, even Logan could sing it.

In one blinding instant, Logan connected, saw the flickering images in her mind and nearly doubled over from the force of her pain.

The nurse put her hand on Logan's shoulder and he swung around, startled. She held up a syringe and he nodded, then watched her insert the needle into the port, push the plunger, and deploy the sedative.

Grace's body slowly went slack.

He left her after a few minutes and went to confer with the team. He'd finally seen into her mind, and had something to work with. But they informed him he only had four hours until the sedation wore off.

#

Logan helped himself to a new, untraceable cell phone and a set of car keys from the cabinet beside the elevator. As he emerged into daylight at ground level, he punched in a number he knew by heart.

"Sarah speaking."

"Brontosaurus here. She's in trouble and needs your help."

"Where is she?"

"I'll pick you up in front of your building." He glanced at his watch. "Thirty minutes."

"It'll take me forty to get there."

"Where are you?"

When she answered, he plugged the address into

his GPS. "Perfect. I'm nearly on your doorstep. Ten minutes."

"Fine."

The way she'd responded to his call without question, convinced him she was somehow involved in the same thing Grace was. But knowing she was a psychologist, he'd keep his cards close just in case she was bluffing.

When he pulled up in front of a quaint little yellow house, the door opened and Sarah quick-stepped down the walk and hopped into the car. "I'm being watched."

Interesting. And he noted that she wore sensible shoes, jeans with a knife-like pleat, and several layers on top, including a navy blue rain jacket: exactly how a woman on the run should be prepared. She even had a shoulder satchel that looked like it could hold a week's worth of clothes and maybe a meal or two.

He pushed a couple of buttons on the phone before sliding it into a holder on the dash and pulling away from the curb. He tapped the phone, said, "One, six, dash, four, three, Alfa, Charlie," and waited for the response through his earpiece.

When it came, he replied with a simple. "Affirmative," touched the phone again to disconnect, then looked at Sarah. "You ever done this before?"

She shrugged. "Depends on what it is we're doing."

"Losing a tail." He'd already noticed the silver Pathfinder making the same three turns he'd just made. "We'll drive for a while, draw them in, then redirect. Do you know who they are? Why they're watching you?"

"Not exactly."

"What *do* you know?"

"In regards to what?" she hedged.

"Cut the crap, Sarah." He sucked in a breath while he tried to get a handle on his temper. "I told you Grace is in serious trouble. My gut says you're the key to helping her, and I hope you can be trusted because whatever's going on is big and it's ugly."

Sarah watched his face. "*They*," she said using air quotes, "don't know anything about me. My identity is well-protected. They think I'm just her friend. They have no clue about our connection and don't know that I've helped her get through the stuff she hasn't told them about. Mostly stuff from—"

"From her childhood."

Her eyes narrowed. "Yes."

"So she trusts you completely?"

"Yes and no. She's shared her history. Everything up until she started traveling with Isaac. She said she couldn't tell me about that part of her life. Said it was for my protection. So I don't know who *they* are."

He took a deep breath. "Do you speak any languages besides English?"

"Not exactly."

"Vague answers are no help to me *or* to Grace right now."

She was quick. "Look, I can't converse, but I understand key phrases, stuff that's useful, in half a dozen languages. I can usually get the gist if someone speaks slowly. But I do sign fluently, if that's any help to you."

"Not yet."

"Tell me where she is and what's going on.

"She's hidden. She's physically safe. But mentally... I'm not so sure. She's singing... In French."

Sarah covered her mouth. "Shit."

Logan pressed on. "We've only got a few hours until the sedative wears off. They don't want to give her another one unless they absolutely have to." He went on to tell Sarah everything he could about Grace's condition, the drug implants, and what he had seen when it all wore off.

When Sarah asked him to describe the man Grace had freaked out at when she was waking up, Logan quickly reeled off the description. "White male, mid-forties, five-ten, athletic build, gray hair, gray beard, tanned skin, brown eyes, blue shirt, white lab coat."

Sarah held up a hand. "Got it." She leaned her head back against the seat. "I have to get to her quickly."

"Should take less than forty minutes to shake the tail and get clear."

Half an hour later, within a vast industrial area, he pulled up to a security gate, used a key fob to make it slide open, then drove into an open warehouse. After the door rattled down behind them, he told her to leave her jacket in the car and follow him. He led her through a maze of crates and cargo skids to the far side of the building where a tiny bumblebee helicopter sat on a trailer. Logan held out a hand to help her up onto the deck and into the bird.

Meanwhile, the car they'd arrived in was backed out of the warehouse and driven to the farthest exit, where it accessed the interstate, southbound. The man and woman in the car looked remarkably like Logan and Sarah, the backseat passenger was a woman who resembled Grace.

Ten strained and silent minutes passed before the helicopter pilot showed up. He and Logan pulled the trailer out into an enclosed yard, boarded the tiny craft and they were soon airborne, barely skimming over buildings, then trees, until landing in a deserted farmyard.

The copter zipped away as soon as Sarah and Logan disembarked and scurried to an outbuilding where a small family-style van was stored.

Sarah climbed into the back and hid herself on the floor while Logan drove. For the ten minute ride, she pondered the cloak-and-dagger moves, impressed there seemed to be great preparation and no lack of funds.

When the van stopped, Logan helped her out into a run-of-the-mill residential garage.

She followed him past bicycles, a lawn mower, and a collection of garden tools, through a door, down two flights of stairs, and into a brightly lit room containing nothing but a dozen golf carts. He chose one, used a security card to start it, and she sat dumbfounded, watching a wall slide quietly away to reveal a long white tunnel.

She was at a loss for words while Logan drove them through a myriad of breezeways until they reached a dead-end.

He climbed out of the cart, and she followed him to another blank wall. She saw no buttons, no electric eye, nothing, but still, after just a few moments, the wall slid open and Logan led her into what seemed to be a perfectly normal, everyday hospital ward.

She blinked, and gawked, feeling a bit like Alice gone down the rabbit hole.

Chapter 14

Sarah scanned the hallway, noting the textured material on the ceiling and upper walls which would account for the noticeable lack of sound. Even their footsteps on the polished tile seemed muted. Creepy.

They'd reached Grace's room without seeing a single person. The place appeared to be deserted, yet there was the faintest hum of human energy.

Sarah's heart bumped and sank at the sight of Grace, so still, so colorless, so empty, stretched almost flat on the hospital bed with tubes and leads running from her to the machines lining the wall behind her.

Her hair had been slicked back, pulled away from her face in two neat braids. The grayish purple of the sunken skin around her eyes was accentuated by the frightening pale slackness of the rest of her face.

Logan stroked Grace's shoulder and Sarah noted the myriad of emotions flitting across his face. The man was invested, big time.

He glanced at his watch. "Sedation should be wearing off soon," he said, as he dragged two chairs close to the bed.

"I need to be alone with her," said Sarah.

He hesitated, shrugged. "I'll leave, but the room's

monitored by the medical staff, and I'll be watching with them.

A nurse entered, nodded to Logan, then spoke to Sarah. "I'll be standing by with medication if she needs it."

"She won't need it. I'll be able to convince her she's safe."

"I believe you, but I have to stay. I won't get in your way." She moved to the far corner of the room and settled into a chair.

Sarah was sorry she had to banish Logan, but didn't want a man in the room. She wished she dared touch him to give him some comfort, but his connection to Grace served as a warning that he might be able to read others as well, and Sarah couldn't afford to let anyone connect while she worked on freeing Grace's mind from the memories terrorizing her.

Because he still hovered, she gave him more. "I think I understand how you're feeling, Logan. But you need to remember that you brought me here to help her, so you have to trust me and let me handle her my way. She'll be utterly exhausted by the continuous use of sedation. Drugs don't allow the mind to process and file as it does in sleep. As it needs to in order for her to recuperate from whatever set her off. My goal is to coax her to relax naturally so she can get the sleep she needs to heal."

Tension flashed across his shoulders, into his jaw, and throughout the very essence of the man. "I hear what you're saying, and I hope to Christ you can reach her before…"

He shook his head and in silence sent one last

message to the still figure in the bed. *It's your turn now Grace. Touch me.*

#

Logan chose a station just inside the door of the control room, keyed in his personal access code, and chose Grace's room number from the menu. He slipped on headphones and waited.

Frustration rippled when Dr. Kelton stepped into her room and switched off the audio feed while he spoke to Sarah. Their meeting was very brief. It appeared they each had something important to say, each responded with something akin to surprise, then Kelton reactivated the microphones and left the room.

It took another long twenty minutes before Grace stirred. Minutes in which he watched Sarah undo the braids and spread Grace's hair out on the pillow, stroke her face, and her arms. He wondered about the tapping she did on the inside of Grace's wrist while humming an unfamiliar tune. Logan cranked up the volume to be sure it wasn't the song Grace had been singing the last time she'd been awake.

While he watched, he pondered the relationship between the two women. They seemed closer than counselor and patient. Speculation had him reading ownership on Sarah's face, in her movements. Thinking back, he realized she'd sounded possessive when they'd talked about Grace in the car.

Before he could open a search window on the computer at the next station, the electronics attached to Grace began to signal changes. Lights blinked on monitors and Sarah leaned over Grace, blocking his view.

#

Grace opened her eyes, focused slowly, and smiled when she recognized Sarah. Relief and warmth washed through her as she was drawn into arms she knew, allowing herself to be held by the one person she trusted. With her past. With her self.

"He's here," she whispered to Sarah.

"Who?"

"He's not dead. I saw him."

Sarah edged back to look into Grace's eyes. "He is dead, Grace. You didn't see him. You saw someone who looks a little like he did."

"When I woke up he was here, leaning over me, telling me it was okay."

She enunciated with care. "It was not him."

Grace desperately needed Sarah to understand the danger. "It was." She struggled to sit up, get up, needed to run, but Sarah placed a hand firmly on either side of her face and forced her to be still, commanded her attention.

"You were coming off powerful drugs and you mistakenly thought it was him. The man you saw is the doctor who's been helping you."

Grace became more insistent. "He said he would help me. I remember when he said that. Said he would prove I could dance. I just had to try harder, my muscles had to be molded, become more feminine, I had to learn to feel like a woman feels when...." Her vision blurred.

Sarah was shaking her and her voice sounded far away. "Grace. Do you want to get well or would you rather stay drugged for the rest of your life?"

"I'm afraid."

"Of course you are, but you've been afraid before, dammit. Let go of the past so I can help you learn to live again."

Grace could feel the vibration of her voice. It felt odd. "He said he would make me pay. He said Isaac—"

Logan knocked loudly on the door before striding into the room.

Grace's eyes were wide with a look of confusion as a single word slipped from her lips. "Brontosaurus."

He didn't answer, just took her hand in his and stared into her eyes, willing the confusion and uncertainty away, while demanding she listen to his thoughts.

Sarah eased out of the way.

Logan projected his internal voice. *Listen to me Grace.*

She stared at him.

He clasped both her hands in one of his and held his other one out to her, palm up. She looked at it, studied the strong fingers and thought, *touch me.*

Ah, there you are.

She blinked in surprise, her eyes widening.

Where do you want me to touch you Grace?

Everywhere. I need to feel your skin on mine.

Later, when we're alone.

Touch me now, Logan. I want your hands on me.

Sarah cleared her throat and they both looked at her. "I'm not sure why you thought you needed me, Logan."

He gave her a sideways look. "You, too?"

She smiled. "Only her. I can't hear you."

Bloody good thing, he thought. "Okay, I needed

you because she needs you. I can connect, but you know the hell she's been through. You can help her, coach her through the fear."

"Excuse me, but I'm still in the room."

"Sorry, new habit." Logan smiled at her. "I've gotten used to talking over and around you in the last few days."

"Fine, but I'm awake now, so could someone please tell me where I am, why I'm here, and what the hell's going on?"

Surprised at the instant change of tone, Logan muttered, "A little snappy all of a sudden?"

Sarah laughed. "One thing you'll learn about our Grace is when she's nervous or uncertain, she hisses and spits. Eventually, you'll recognize the attack as a cover-up. Why don't you leave us alone for a little while so we can talk about what's going on?"

Logan didn't envy Sarah the job of getting Grace to relax. "I'll be down the hall." As he reached for the door he looked back at them and said, "I should remind you, there's no such thing as absolute privacy in this building."

Yes, he thought, that would be inconvenient for them.

Chapter 15

Grace's tension melted into need when the door closed behind Logan. "Sarah," she whispered. "I'm scared."

Sarah leaned in, wrapped her arms around Grace and held her while minutes and apprehension slipped away like sand in an hourglass.

Sarah's voice soothed her. "It's okay baby. We're going to get everything back to normal real soon, I promise you."

Grace still couldn't manage more than a thin whisper. "I thought it was him."

Sarah stroked her hair. "He's dead, Grace. I know with absolute certainty that he can't ever hurt you again."

"I was so sure it was him leaning over me, smiling in that secret way, you know? But you're absolutely, positively, *certain* it was the doctor?"

Sarah drew back far enough for Grace to see the honesty in her eyes. "Baby, I spoke with Dr. Kelton less than thirty minutes ago. He's a man in his forties, barely ten years older than you. If Monsieur were still alive, he'd be at least sixty or seventy by now. But I assure you," she hesitated and then delivered each word individually. "He. Is. Dead."

Grace nodded, the simple logic and Sarah's confidence helped to ease the grip of the old nightmare, so she could contemplate the here and now. "What's going on, Sarah? Why am I here, hooked up to all these machines?" She turned to scrutinize the wall lined with electronic gadgetry. "This is more than just a hospital, isn't it?"

Sarah stayed seated on the bed, one of Grace's hands held firmly between her own. "Let's start with how you got here. What's the last thing you remember before you woke up in a hospital the first time?"

Grace laid her head back against the pillows and closed her eyes, giving some thought to the fact the room was being monitored. She kept her voice carefully steady when she finally began to speak.

"I was with Logan. At my place. I had a splitting headache. Needed meds." *A handful.* "But I was making tea first." *Stupid. Trying to be normal.* "That's the last thing I remember." *The last thing I want to remember.*

Sarah shook her head, trying to sort the words and thoughts coming to her interwoven, jumbled together. "What kind of meds?"

"Just the usual. Well the strongest of the usual, actually." *Even they don't work anymore.*

"Names?"

"Don't know." *Don't want to know. Pick a color, mix and match, who the hell cares?*

Sarah's eyebrows rose slightly. "You take drugs strong enough to knock you out and you don't know what they are?"

"Affirmative." *Back off.*

No. "Talk to me, Grace."

"*No.*"

"Grace."

She fisted a handful of bed sheet. "When the pain fucking consumes me, I take anything I can get. I'd rather be unconscious than endure daggers piercing the suffocating sludge in my head. If I stay awake until the puking starts, I pray for death." She inhaled dramatically. "The old quack set me up with a whole cabinet full of different stuff to try. He keeps tabs on how much I use, tells me how to mix them effectively."

"How long have you been doing this?"

"Doing what?"

"Keeping me in the dark. Taking drugs, filtering your thoughts. Blocking me."

"They're my thoughts."

"Grace."

"Since Isaac died."

Sarah looked like she wanted to yell. To demand to know why Grace had kept secrets from her, not said anything about the pain or the medication. Instead, she appeared to shove her anger onto a back burner before she asked, "Do you remember much about the time right after Isaac's death? About the hospital?"

"When I woke up, he told me about Isaac. Said I'd been kept sedated because I was hysterical. Said I'd probably have headaches for a while. I told him that wouldn't be anything new; headaches were a part of my everyday life. The doctor said he could help me. Quizzed me for a while, sent me for a scan of some kind, implanted something to release a chemical, to balance my system. He said it'd keep the pain at a minimum, then gave me bunch other stuff to take.

Claimed it was all cutting edge therapy used in Europe for prevention of Post-Traumatic Stress Disorder. Prevents flashbacks."

So you knew about the implants.

Yeah. I get new ones every six months.

Jesus Grace. "Why didn't you tell me?"

"They're just headaches, Sarah, not a brain tumor like I thought before so no big deal. I can live with a little pain. I've watched enough people cope with PTSD, I didn't want to go there myself."

Sarah looked into the eyes of an innocent victim and said softly, "They were keeping you drugged so your memories would stay safely locked away. You know something, Grace."

"I don't understand." But, yet... she did. Fragments of the nightmare hovering in her peripheral vision for several years were moving into full view. The picture still made no sense but it would. She knew it would because, like a giant jigsaw puzzle, once all the edges were in place, the center would come together swiftly.

"Someone has gone to a great deal of trouble to keep you in the dark when, to my way of thinking, it would have been much simpler to kill you."

Grace's jaw dropped and she gasped out, "Sarah!"

"Sorry, baby, but it's a horrible truth you have to face."

Somehow, from the depths of a secret place in her mind, she already knew. And in that knowing, came the realization that her life *was* in danger now. Her memories were no longer being repressed so very soon she'd know what it was she'd seen or heard. What it was Dr. Kusavinski was trying to keep her from knowing.

Sarah looked around the room to find the camera lens, but saw nothing she could identify. Deciding audio was just as good she said, "Hey, Logan, I think it's time for your input."

His disembodied voice seemed to come out of the walls. "What can I do for you?"

Sarah frowned. "Nice. The invisible man. Okay for the ugly guys, but you're not exactly hard to look at."

Grace tried to match Sarah's light-hearted tone. "Could you please come in here? I hate talking to the air."

#

Logan attempted to keep the frown off his face while he spent twenty minutes explaining the details of what had happened—how and why Grace had ended up in the ETC Medical Centre several days after collapsing in her home. The bottom line being, her emotional and physical state had been manipulated by the chemical implants, which kept her dependent on the other drugs.

"Are you saying they made me a drug addict?"

"According to Dr. Kelton, no. The implants themselves were creating the headaches when certain suppressed memories were triggered. Now that you scan clean, the medical team anticipates no drug dependency. But to be on the safe side, they'll be keeping you under their care for another ten days before they give you a clean bill and consider you not at risk."

"Ten *days*? You can't keep me trapped in here that long."

He sighed. This wasn't going to be easy. It was almost laughable how far from easy it would be to keep a woman like Grace from leaving if she wanted to. He didn't envy Kelton his job. "With your memory no longer repressed, your life is probably in danger." He looked at Sarah. "You're also at risk, and therefore, a guest here until it's safe to leave."

Sarah's gaze was steady. "I understood the implication."

"So now what?" Grace's eyes had darkened to burnished gold. "What the hell do we do?"

He stuffed his hands in his pockets. "Once the medics are certain you're not physiologically drug dependent, you'll be moved to a private suite here in the facility for a short time, then we'll get you into a safe house for a while."

"How long?"

"For as long as it takes to make sure you're out of danger."

Grace knew the answer, but felt better for asking the question. "And how will you know when I'm no longer in danger?"

"Once your memory is tapped, you'll mean little to them."

Them? Who's them?

He smiled. "We don't know yet, but we're working on it."

"And how exactly are you going to tap my memory?"

"Dr. Kelton has all sorts of tools."

A quick macabre picture of a room filled with

hammers, saws and drills flitted through Grace's mind. Logan laughed. "I'm talking much more civilized. The team will come in and explain everything to you, and Sarah will be with you at all times."

Sarah took that as her opening. "Are you talking hypnosis?"

"According to the medical team, hypnosis would be the preferred option. Drugs are another, but considering Grace's chemistry—or more importantly, the previous assault on her chemical balance—they'd like to avoid that. We have an extraordinary staff here and they'll explain all their ideas to you."

Grace watched Sarah's face and was satisfied when she saw caution but no distrust there. And her own uneasy prickles of warning eased. Just one problem lingered. "Logan, the doctor with the gray beard."

"Yes?"

"I don't want to see him again."

"Dr. Kelton is a good man and quite concerned about you."

"I'm sorry, but he reminds me of someone."

Logan glanced away for just a moment saying quietly, "We connected those dots."

"And," Sarah interjected quickly, "Dr. Kelton has spent the last half hour removing his beard. He told me he didn't want anything to interfere with your recovery."

"Oh, well, he didn't have to."

"Yes, I think he did," said Sarah. "As the head man on your case, he can't afford to have you afraid of him. Didn't want anything to get in the way of your recovery."

Logan managed a smile. "Don't worry, Grace. It's just hair. It'll grow back."

There was something different in Logan's expression. *Something else is wrong. What is it?* She sent out the thought and listened intently for his answering voice to slip into her mind—but nothing happened. She watched him. Tried again. *What's wrong?*

Logan changed his own thoughts like slipping in a new disc. He formed a mental picture of his hands on her shoulders, drawing her toward him. He allowed a small opening, just enough to allow her to see, and smiled when he heard her quick intake of breath.

Sarah watched the body language, not needing to hear the thoughts that passed between them. "Starting to feel like a fifth wheel here."

"Sorry."

"Actually, it's perfect timing. Doctor Kelton wanted to consult with me and now seems like a good time to leave you two alone for a bit." She gave Logan a look he interpreted as a warning. "Remember, what Grace needs most is sleep."

"I'll help her with that," he replied.

"I'll hold you to it." Her slow steady look, left him in no doubt she was serious.

Logan followed her to the door and switched off the light when she'd left.

Darkness blanketed the room, leaving only a colorful glow from the electronics.

"What are you doing?" Grace demanded.

"Giving us the closest thing to privacy we can get in here." He leaned over, brushed a soft kiss across her forehead.

Something was off about him. She suspected he hadn't shared all the information. He'd held back a detail or two. She'd have to see if she could drag it out of him. "What's wrong?"

"Nothing's wrong, Grace." His lips grazed hers, but with tenderness and a distinct absence of passion.

She took hold of his shirt and pulled him toward her, damning the darkness, wishing she could see the expression in his eyes. She whispered, "You, are lying to me. You're worried. And I think you're angry, too. Is it about the procedures? The implants? The people involved? The ones who did this to me?"

"All of that and more." He ran his fingertips along her jaw. His hand settled against her throat. "It wasn't easy finding you nearly dead, seeing you half-crazed, learning someone had manipulated you and interfered with your mind." He shook his head. "It's been a rough couple of days watching your terror."

And then she knew. With the suddenness of a bullet, the knowledge was inside of her. Her voice went flat. "So you saw everything. You helped yourself to all my memories. My secrets. You had no right." Cold seeped under her skin and she let go of his shirt.

Logan wove a psychic wall of protection around his thoughts to prevent her from seeing the truth.

"All I saw was your terror, combined with a white-hot flash of a photo-like memory of a bearded man leaning over you."

She softened for a moment, touched his face. "It was a very long time ago and I don't want to talk about it."

"Hey." He shrugged. "I understand. It's private.

Not something you need to share. Luckily, the quick visual was enough for me to figure out Kelton's appearance was setting you off." He could feel the change in the air. He'd somehow given himself away. New tension was building inside her and he had no idea what to do about it. He became still, waited for her to blast him.

"Logan, you're a cop. Don't you have memories of situations you'd like to forget?"

"Sure," he said cautiously.

"Well, so do I. Can we leave it at that?" Her fingertips teased his mouth. "Tuck it away, Logan. Far, far, away. And then, for God's sake, would you kiss me properly?"

Constantly amazed by this woman, he shook his head, then asked with an edge of wonder, "Where does your strength come from?" He slid both hands into her hair. His mouth settled over hers, hungry, wanting.

Her arms wound around his neck, eliminating any space left between them. "Hmmmm," she murmured. "Much better already."

He half laughed against her mouth, muttered, "Shut up, Grace," and poured all his energy into making her forget about everything but him.

Chapter 16

Sarah had spoken only briefly with Dr. Kelton prior to Grace waking up, but was instantly attracted to something in his bottomless brown eyes. Now, staring at him with his jaunty gray beard gone, she was momentarily speechless.

The man is stunning. A face like that, *and he hides it behind a mask of hair? Probably has to so he'll be taken seriously.* She stifled a smirk.

She couldn't resist teasing him a bit. "Do you feel somewhat vulnerable now, Doctor?" She smiled sweetly.

His focus sharpened with an indignant air. "I don't think you know me well enough to pass judgment."

She worked some innocence into her expression. "Sir, no offence intended. I don't judge people, I observe. It's what I do. You might say it's who I am."

The corner of his mouth twitched. "My dear Dr. Rideout, even with our acquaintance being less than a quarter of an hour in duration, I am quite certain you are much more than an instrument of observation."

She laughed. "Point to you, sir. My name is Sarah."

Only his eyes showed the smile. "And mine's Christopher. Perhaps, Sarah, we should get to the business at hand. Your patient is now also mine. And for her health and well-being we'll need to work together." He handed her a hard-copy of Grace's file. "This contains everything since she arrived here, unconscious. Take some time to read through it, I'll be back in about forty minutes to discuss treatment options."

Sarah had already opened the file and nodded absently as he left the room.

Christopher Kelton went to an observation desk and flicked on the monitor for Grace's room. The picture was quite dark, and the scene intimate. Logan lay stretched out on the bed with Grace curled against him.

Electronic readout numbers across the bottom of the screen indicated Grace was sleeping. The first genuine rest she'd had in days. He smiled, pleased at her progress. And progress meant hope, hope that irreparable damage had not been done to her mind and she would experience a full recovery.

But he also hoped he wasn't being prematurely optimistic based on the strength she'd shown in surviving her childhood trauma. Would it be too much to add the burden of the circumstances surrounding Isaac's death?

Hearing someone approaching, Kelton pressed a key to change the image on the monitor. Agent Williams stopped behind him, studied the pretty blond on the screen, and asked, "Who's the woman?"

"Grace's therapist." He checked his watch. "We have a consult in half an hour."

"Then what?"

"Then we find out what the next move will be.

They're making the choices. We'll give them all the control we can. Grace needs to feel like she's choosing to participate."

"Even though she's a prisoner?"

Kelton frowned, turning in his chair to face the other man. "She's not a prisoner."

"What she's not... is free to go," he said without inflection of opinion, as though the words themselves were enough.

"We've been treating her medically and will move on to psychological support. Meanwhile, she's under our protection."

"Yeah, but she's not allowed to leave until the psychological support has mined the information she's hiding."

"She's not hiding it voluntarily," stated Kelton with just an edge of annoyance creeping into his voice.

"You sure about that? Are you positive once the drugs wear off she'll tell you everything? What about her family loyalties? Won't they affect her judgment? Are you absolutely certain she's an innocent in this? Ever consider it might just be a role she's playing?" prodded Williams.

"You've got to be the most suspicious bastard I know. I bet you don't crack an egg without wondering first if it's been tampered with."

"Keeps me alive in this business, Kelton. Keeps me alive."

"Why all the interest in a case you're not assigned to?"

"Yet. My department will act on any information she gives up."

Kelton pinned him with a look. "It's more than

that and we both know it."

"You ever get tired of shrinking heads?" he muttered, then shrugged. "I've got a feeling she's a link to something—else. Something connected to me. Can't put my finger on it yet, but I will."

Kelton smiled. "Not like you to sound uncertain, Williams. You starting to tap into the spidey senses you insist you don't have?"

Williams stared at him for a beat or two, blinked, and said, "Hey, you shaved off your beard."

"Observant, aren't you?"

"I need to know how long until you get some solid information from her about Isaac's background and contacts."

Kelton almost smiled at the man's avoidance tactics. "I'm anticipating some kind of progress within forty-eight hours."

"Make it thirty-six."

"This isn't a negotiation. We're dealing with a delicate mind here. Stick to your own department and go shoot a spy or something. I'll call you day after tomorrow." He slipped the earphones on and leaned back in his chair.

Williams grumbled while he left the room and headed for the elevator. He hated dealing with head doctors. Maybe a trip to the range would take the edge off his nerves. Working through a half dozen simulations certainly couldn't hurt.

#

Furious with herself, Sarah leaned back in the chair. *How did I miss this volume of drugs? I must be a complete idiot. Hours and hours, entire days with her, and I never saw it. Never even suspected. Just put it all down to—*

Dr. Kelton entered the office, moving as silently as a cat. He stopped beside her chair. When she glanced up and met his gaze, his fingertips touched her shoulder and he smiled. His fingers slid down as though to grip her shoulder, but didn't, and he moved to take the chair beside her instead.

"Well, what do you think?" he asked in a voice so low and sexy she found herself entranced, inexplicably captivated, unable to look away.

His expression became almost sleepy and her heart actually fluttered.

"Sarah? What do you think of the history there?" Without breaking eye contact, he tipped his head toward the file. "Had you suspected anything at all about Grace's drug use?"

She shook her head, struggling to put words together. "I was so blind. You must think I'm an idiot."

"Don't be too hard on yourself." His voice was soothing, like the stroke of a hand. "They created a remarkable product. She was able to function at an acceptable level and seem normal in every way, but anything that triggered certain memories also triggered the headaches. Through pain-stimulated subconscious suggestion, they programmed her to unknowingly activate the implants herself."

"Programmed her? Hypnosis? Mind control? How the hell did they pull that off?"

"After her father's death she was kept sedated for several days. Did you see her then?"

"No. It was very complicated. Between surgery to repair her arm and hospital transfers, I somehow missed her, and it was nearly four days before I caught up. She was still sedated."

"Hospital transfers?"

Sarah hated she'd been so easily duped. "I guess that's it. At first I'd assumed I'd received the wrong information. Then I thought her mother, a world-famous entertainer, had been playing games to keep the paparazzi at bay. But now I see it was all part of an entirely different scenario, wasn't it?"

He nodded. "While she was in their care, the implants were settled and the programming implemented. A very sophisticated operation, it would appear. Now we are left to wonder why she was targeted."

Sarah bit at the inside of her cheek. "This kind of sophistication is far beyond my scope, and therefore I can't possibly comment on it. But what I can tell you is that in the years since, Grace hasn't exhibited any unusual memory gaps. She talks to me at least twice a week, not always intense therapy of course, but I've never had so much as an inkling of anything psychologically amiss. Her lack of memory from the day Isaac died is a normal psychosomatic reaction."

"She lost the entire day?"

"Yes. But I should tell you, from the moment she got up that morning, her every thought was about her upcoming evening performance of Renaissance, so I didn't find it the least bit unusual for her to have lost the whole day and not just her memory of the events surrounding Isaac's death."

"Does anyone else know of your relationship?"

Sarah's eyebrows lifted and her mouth twitched. "What do you mean by *relationship*?"

He didn't even blink. "The fact you have the same mother, the famous Meredith." He watched her face. "What, no surprise?"

She smiled. "Why would I be surprised? I've known for years."

"And how long has Grace known?"

"Since she was eighteen. I had to wait until then to tell her. Did you figure it out on your own or use DNA?"

He smiled then. "Like you, Dr. Rideout, I am a trained observer." He hesitated just long enough to make her curious. "And a scientist."

She began to smile back at him, but the sudden intensity of his gaze made her heart flutter again and it seemed as though his voice was very far away.

"Sarah?" He was leaning toward her, his fingertips resting lightly on her knee while she stared up into his eyes. "Are you feeling alright?"

The smoothness of melted dark chocolate. It was there in his voice again, and she could almost taste it.

"I think we should discuss Grace's therapy now. Do you trust me, Sarah?"

She heard herself reply, "Of course Dr. Kelton," and wondered about the huskiness in her words.

"Please." He held out his hand, palm up and she placed her own against it. His fingers closed. He smiled, and his voice dropped an octave. "Call me Christopher."

During the next two hours, Sarah agreed to convince Grace to undergo extreme and extended hypnotherapy, pledging herself a part of the team.

She'd debrief Grace, and endorse any and all suggestions made by the man she'd been staring at, mesmerized by.

When she left his office, Sarah made her way through the hallways, barely noticing the shiny floors, the paintings on the walls, the engraved plaques, or the discrete directional signs. Her mind was stuck back there in Christopher's office. She tried to mentally dissect their conversation, analyze what had happened. When, and how.

She shook her head as though to bring herself out of a fog.

She had agreed with everything he'd said, followed along with his outline of treatment, had felt herself nodding. Yet she remembered little of the content. Only the image of his eyes, the dark chocolate color matching the richness of his voice. The tiny crinkles at the outer edges, the kind that came from laughter and sunshine. And his mouth. *Jesus,* just the thought of his mouth was making her warm all over.

Professional, Sarah. You are a professional, for heaven's sake. Her thoughts began to gel enough to create a pattern for her to follow. She stepped into a ladies' room, splashed cold water on her face, stared at herself in the mirror, and delivered a brief lecture.

"You are not a silly teenager. You are a respected psychologist. The FBI uses *your* profiling skills, *your* perfectly-objective and highly-educated opinions to solve crimes that baffle most law enforcement agencies."

She drew a long deep breath, let it out slowly, and squinted into the mirror. "I do believe I've been very professionally played, one move at a time." She swung around, surveying the room for cameras. "And if by chance you are listening, *Christopher*?" The corner of her mouth twitched. "Dr. Kelton. I applaud you. But it's only fair for me to say that I've always found the game of chess quite boring, so perhaps you could think of something a little more... stimulating for next time." She winked into the mirror and left the room.

Dr. Christopher Kelton, esteemed commander of an entire division of ETC, sitting alone in his office, threw back his head and laughed as he hadn't in years, then reached over and turned off the video monitor.

Chapter 17

It was early morning and Grace wasn't really asleep. Many, many years ago, more like a lifetime now, she'd learned the art of feigning sleep. She could even dupe the machines. Hell, she'd developed enough control over her heart rate and respiration that she could appear to be unconscious, while fully able to use all of her senses. Yes, even her eyes. Staring blankly, looking glazed over, she could step away from the pain and still see what she wanted to see. Old familiar words slipped into her head, "And if you can endure, with just the faintest of smiles on your face, well, then you have mastered it all... the control... the ability to survive anything."

Sarah and Logan stood near the door talking. Too far away. Sounds filtered through her head, but she couldn't quite make out the words. She let her mind open, listened for their thoughts. Waited.

Nothing. She wanted to frown, to open her eyes and ask them what was wrong but she didn't. And grew frustrated, waiting.

The door opened, closed, and there was silence, the void made her shudder. She was alone. Uneasy. Something felt off, but she didn't know what. There was a niggling of memory, a tugging of thought. She wanted to remember, to let the pictures flow into her consciousness, but held herself in check. They said all the implants were gone. The cold wash of fear threatened.

What if the memories *were* too much? What if the old weasel was right? They would tear at her, strip her down all over again. Leave her broken like the others. She recognized the tap-tapping of her heart and hated that the drug wouldn't be dispatched to automatically calm her. She'd have to do it the old way.

She concentrated on the rhythm of her heart, forcing space between the taps, compelling them to slow, deepen into thumps, slowing the motion now to *kathump.. kathump..* slower.. *kaaathump..* slower... much.. much.... slower..... *Kaaaathuummpp*, a gentle swooshing, sighing, slow motion, barely discernible sound now... *kaaaaathhhhuuuummmmpp.*

And then silence.

Her thoughts drifted softly at first. *She* wasn't one of them. She *had* survived. She had already survived everything. Hadn't she? Hadn't she stood in front and told her truth? Hadn't she walked away psychologically intact? Proud of herself and Isaac for what they had done? And hadn't she finally stepped onto the stage whole—fluid, elegant, and totally engulfed in her own serenity while she'd danced with him?

He had choreographed *Renaissance*. She had overcome her terror of the song. She hadn't broken, fallen into a graceless heap. She'd boldly let her eyes move past the edge of the stage. And when they'd stood at the center of the dance floor for the audience to celebrate their performance she'd looked directly into the eyes of every person in the front row.

It was her own finale, her own triumph, and Isaac had stepped back, bowing to her. He had given her strength, and then he had given her the praise that meant more than anything. She'd walked into his arms and known an unbelievably sweet euphoria. Her spirit was finally free.

Another   whispered *kaaaaaathhhhuuuuummmmmpp*

Mere hours later, they had taken him from her. Men wearing uniforms had ripped him out of her arms and taken him. But he'd already been gone. The light, she'd seen it leaving his eyes when he asked her why the music had stopped right in the middle of such a beautiful song. So she'd sung for him, finished the song, and watched the light that was him, evaporate, vanish with one last puff of warm steamy breath in cold air. Isaac's soul had left her before the end of the song. But she had promised him she'd continue.

Promised.

She felt the tingling begin in her fingertips. Heart rate too low, she thought vaguely.

The promise. Shock rocketed through her body leaving her oblivious to the tingling, the enveloping hum of cells seeking oxygen.

She had forgotten the promise she'd made to him. But now she remembered. And she must let him know. She must tell him she was sorry and would put it right, but he seemed so far away.

Isaaaac. She called silently. *Isaaaac, please listen to me. I am so sorry, Isaac. They took it from me, but now my way is clear and I will continue.*

Isaaaac. Please listen to me. I will continue. I can do nothing less.

She could hear the song, softly now, in her head. She followed the words, knowing exactly when, waiting for the moment when his soul had slipped away. *I can't finish it tonight, I am too tired to sing. I need to rest now, Isaac. If I could just rest my head against your shoulder again.* She felt the warmth of him under her cheek, the strength of his arms around her, and she sighed.

He stroked her hair and said softly, "*You forgot your promise, baby.*"

He jerked away when the door was flung open and the room filled with people.

Irritated, annoyed to be interrupted right now, Grace absorbed the scene, could hear an alarm, a buzzing noise somewhere far away—or perhaps nearby—and wondered why nobody turned it off. The doctor and nurses leaned over her, their voices full of concern, sharp instructions, orders. Logan and Sarah were there, watching, looking horrified.

Four beautiful men, tall, dark, silent men, stood at the foot of her bed. They wore white. Orderlies to assist, she supposed. Their eyes watched hers. She was intrigued by the peacefulness in their faces, but distracted by the voices beside her.

Arrest? Who were they arresting? What's going on? Oh. Sweet Jesus, that hurt. What the—. Stop it. That hurts, you moron. Logan. Logan, make them stop dammit. Logan, help me. Sarah, don't let them do this. Ow, shit. Sarah.

And then she heard him inside her head.

Grace, breathe, for God's sake. Breathe.

Logan, make them stop.
Take a breath, just one and they will.
No. Make them leave me alone.

The doctor was gripping her jaw, trying to force her mouth open, to insert an airway, but she stayed grimly clenched, fighting with every ounce. They couldn't make her. She'd never open her mouth for them. They couldn't make her do it.

Dr. Kelton asked for the trach kit. He told Logan he'd have to cut a hole in her throat to force air into her, and then the machine would breathe for her.

Nooo. I don't want to.

Logan stepped to the foot of the bed, between the orderlies, slipped his hand under the covers and grabbed her foot. Staring into her vacant eyes he drove his thumb between the bones of her first two toes and ruthlessly dug his fingers into the arch. He squeezed hard and concentrated on her mind.

Breathe, Grace.

A single tear slipped from the corner of her eye. *Noooo, please don't make me. Oh please, I can't, I don't want to...*

A wheezing sound. No, more of a groan, a sob. She felt her chest heave and the orderlies stepped back as one. Faded away. Vanished.

Logan's hand ran gently up her calf then back to her foot and his fingers slowly, carefully, massaged away the pain he'd caused.

Monitors all around her were making comfortable little noises and she realized the alarm sound had faded. She blinked.

Dr. Kelton's voice was calm when he asked,

"How do you feel?"

She frowned at him. "Like a fucking punching bag."

"Ah, well."

Logan cleared his throat, and managed a half smile. "Nice to see she's still warm and charming. Could I have a little time with her? Alone?"

The room emptied and Grace watched his face while he continued to rub her feet, her ankles. His eyes met hers and his voice was so soft the words themselves startled her. "What the hell was that about?"

When she closed her eyes he raked his fingernails across the soles of her feet and her eyelids flew apart. She gave herself full marks for not trying to physically pull away. "I'm tired, Logan. I want to sleep now."

"Not until you explain."

"What?"

"Explain why you wanted to die." The expression on his face was unreadable. "See, I'm not as stupid as I look. I felt the control, Grace. I know you were blocking. Sarah and I were both trying to get through, but you were completely closed off. What changed your mind?"

"I'm not sure," she lied. She thought of the warmth she'd felt. Wished they hadn't made her come back. It would be so much easier to go with Isaac, be at peace with him. Logan was staring at her, he needed something from her, but she just wanted to close her eyes. "I'm tired."

Logan opened his mouth to argue, to cajole, to ask again, beg for an answer, but the anger edged in, pushed out the concern for her, stomping on the feelings, the wash of emotions when she'd taken that breath. He struggled for nearly a minute and then finally, through clenched teeth, he said, "Have a nice life, Grace," and left the room. He'd had enough. She wasn't worth it. He didn't need to be jerked around by some nut-case with a death wish.

Kelton was waiting in the hall. "Well?"

"Well what?" he ground out.

The doctor tipped his head towards the closed door. "What do you think?"

"I think she's fucking certifiable. She just tried to kill herself with mind control. I'd advise you to keep close tabs on her monitors, and if anything starts to slip even a little, stop her before she gets too far away."

"You're leaving?"

He had no doubt Kelton already knew the answer, but it was easier to play it out as expected. "Yeah. Had enough for a while."

"Didn't figure you for a quitter."

"There's a first time for everything. I need a little distance, air, daylight maybe."

"You're not cleared for topside without changes."

"Yeah, got that." His attempt to laugh lacked enthusiasm. "What the hell, they say a change is better than a rest." Maybe he'd try something drastic this time.

Kelton's parting shot had a ring of apology to it. "She's about to go through some intense therapy. If you aren't signing on to be a part of it," he hesitated for only an instant, "I need you to stay away completely."

Logan wavered. Steeled himself, "How long?"

"Hard to say. Maybe as little as three weeks, or as long as six months. Depends on her progress."

Logan shook his head. "Probably better without me in the way. Take care of her."

He passed Sarah in the hallway and she reached out to grab his arm. "Where you going?"

"Out."

"I thought we were stuck here."

"You are." And with that he walked away.

#

Grace stared at the ceiling. She'd been so close to an escape. Isaac was there, waiting for her. But it hadn't been time. If it had been the right time, no one could have dragged her back.

It was the promise. She couldn't leave until she'd fulfilled the promise.

Once she was whole, she had to save the others, put an end to the evil. Had to at least try. No she had to succeed. Somehow.

She closed her eyes and fought the threatening tears. Tears of frustration and fear. She reached for one of the extra pillows, rolled on her side and hugged it against herself. *How the hell am I going to pull this off?*

"Pull what off?" She hadn't heard the door open. Sarah stood at her bedside, anger and concern both visible on her face. She sat on the side of the bed and waited.

"I'm sorry, Sarah." She could think of nothing else to say.

The blue eyes so like Meredith's, but with

warmth, stared into hers. "I'm going to give you this one, Grace. But another stunt like today, and I'm gone too."

"It wasn't a stunt."

"Like I said, I'm giving you this one. It's over, we move on from here."

Grace took a deep breath, let it out slowly, touched Sarah's hand, and said softly, "I saw Isaac."

"I know." Sarah turned her hand over and when Grace locked fingers with her, she said, "Tell me about the promise."

Shocked, yet not, Grace answered with, "It's complicated."

"Grace."

"I can't do it unless I survive this place *and* have a mind of my own when I walk out. So there's no point talking about it now."

"You won't tell me."

She smiled grimly. "I can't yet."

Sarah sighed. "Dr Kelton wants to work with you this afternoon."

"Good. Might as well find out if *Etcetera* is anything more than another government cloak-and-dagger game." There was a faint sneer on her face.

Sarah shook her head. "You really are a piece of work. You keep up the attitude and we'll see which one of us ends up most closely resembling our mother."

"Ouch."

"Yeah, not like you didn't ask for it."

Chapter 18

Nancy heard footsteps in the hallway, glanced up, and was startled by the sight of a disheveled man approaching her office. Her eyes narrowed as he reached the threshold, she knew that walk. "Hey, handsome, where you been?"

"Working."

"Nice new look." She eyed the long messy red hair, the torn and dirty clothes. "Airline lost your luggage?"

Logan laughed, flopped onto her couch. "Something like that."

"Assuming the outfit is a disguise, don't you think walking into headquarters is a bad idea?"

He grinned. "Got myself picked up by a black and white on a DIP. They brought me in to sleep it off. Flashed my ID at the desk, slipped into an elevator."

"Drunk in Public's not a very inventive idea, but served the purpose, I suppose."

"I thought so."

"Okay, so what's going on? Where's Grace?"

"Classified." His expression never changed when Nancy rolled her eyes. "I can only tell you, you've got her pets to look after for at least another couple of weeks. She said you could take them out to Caroline at Paradise if you like."

"They like it at my place, and I'm rather enjoying them. Dog's not overly smart so the cat abuses him. They make for great entertainment. Better than TV."

He didn't laugh, didn't appear to have anything else to say, so she got up, closed the door, and went to sit beside him.

"What's wrong?"

"Nothing. Everything."

"Ah, she's messing with your head."

His eyes narrowed. "How much do you know about her?"

Nancy smiled. "Little. Yet, somehow, I feel very connected to Grace. Does that make any sense at all?"

"Too much. She trusts you completely?"

"I think so. Is she okay?"

"She's having a breakdown." He hesitated. "But she's in good hands. The best actually, and she's going to be all right in the end."

"What aren't you saying? Something's eating at you."

He stared at her for a few beats before saying, "She's a very frustrating woman."

"Not exactly news."

"I never know when she's going to shut me out. We've got chemistry, I can reach her when nobody else can. She *seems* to trust me and then, *whack*. She mentally hits me between the eyes, closes down, pushes away, will barely acknowledge me."

"Sounds like self-defense to me. She's the kind of woman doesn't want to be leaning on a big strong guy, thinks she should keep you at arm's length just in case."

"But she needs me—"

Nancy's smile was rueful. "And she doesn't *want* to need anybody."

Logan looked thoughtful. "I promised the doctor I'd stay away from her for a few months."

"Probably a very good plan. Let her climb back up on her feet, establish some control in her life, feel a measure of independence again before you complicate her world."

"Yeah."

"So what will you do while you wait?"

"I've got an assignment. It's pedestrian, but it'll keep me occupied and away for a while." He handed her a slip of paper with a name and phone number on it. "You need me or Grace needs me, call this guy. He'll be able to find me."

\#

Kelton studied Sarah's face. "Tell me about Grace, her background, family, Isaac, your connection to her."

She laughed softly, "Condensed version?"

He waited, saying nothing, so finally she began.

"Meredith, our mother, was fourteen the first time she got pregnant. The problem was taken care of swiftly and without remorse. Two years later, she met my dad on spring break in Mexico, and they got married before boarding a plane for home. The marriage wasn't legal as she had used fake ID. Melissa Kay, aged twenty-one, didn't exist. When she found out she was pregnant again, my dad was thrilled and she was in a freaking frenzy. A pregnancy would ruin her career. She'd already been signed by a manager and a record company, and a baby would ruin everything.

"Nobody wanted a teen idol on screen—or anywhere else for that matter—with a huge belly, a wedding ring, or a baby at her breast. Luckily, my father, who was twenty-four and within months of finishing law school, was mortified when she said she wanted a divorce and an abortion.

"Meredith wriggled out of a divorce and the marriage, as the whole thing was a sham. But the baby was very real, and a whole other matter.

"As the story goes, for several months my dad fought tooth-and-nail with Meredith, her parents, the label, and her manager. He refused to let her out of his sight, afraid she'd sneak away to get an abortion. He knew the risks involved. After all, she was a minor. By the time she reached her second trimester, all parties involved signed a contract. Meredith would stay hidden until she delivered, join the new band on tour, and my dad would keep the baby. Lawyers worked out a very neat and tidy agreement. Neither my father nor I could have any contact with Meredith until after my eighteenth birthday. Her career came first."

"You and your father must hate her."

"My dad has nothing but respect for her. In spite of not wanting the child herself, she at no time did anything to jeopardize the baby she carried. She honored their contract to the letter."

Kelton leaned back in his chair, studying Sarah's face. "How'd it work for you?"

She smiled. "Very well. My dad was a smart guy with a backup plan. He knew of a girl in his graduating class who was pregnant, dumped by the boyfriend for refusing to have an abortion, and terrified her career would be over before it started. He approached her with his idea of teaming up. They got married. My stepsister and I always had a parent at home and life was wonderful for many years."

"Until?"

"Until I turned eighteen and found out I had a famous mother and a baby sister."

"Meredith kept Grace."

"Yes. Grace is five years younger than me. By then, society had not only found a place for women raising children without the sanctity of marriage, but people like Meredith were applauded for having the guts to go it alone, take the baby to work with them, be mothers and career women. She used this to her advantage while she was struggling to become established as a mature entertainer no longer drawing the teenage crowd. She dragged Grace to every job for a while, to the sets, studios, and concerts, but eventually found it easier to leave her in hotel rooms with babysitters or tutors and such."

"Did you ever meet Grace as a child?"

"She was thirteen when I found out about her. I read every tabloid, every news article, became a registered Meredith fan in order to get as close as I could to them."

"You never approached her?"

"I tried so many times that Meredith claimed I was stalking her and got a restraining order. I had to wait until Grace was eighteen before I could meet her and tell her about us."

"How'd she take the news?"

Sarah chuckled. "With great relief."

"Why's that?"

"Grace is special, extremely gifted. And troubled by information she doesn't understand." She smiled to herself. "She knew I existed, had heard my thoughts many times when I'd managed to get close enough to catch a glimpse of her, but didn't know who I was or why she felt so connected to someone she'd never met."

"You couldn't hear her thoughts? I understood you had abilities as well."

"Grace was a natural, born gifted, or as she often says, cursed. I had to learn to read her. Although I must have been born with the ability, I had never tapped into it."

"And now? Is it only Grace, or are you able to connect with others?"

"When Grace wants me to, I hear her thoughts as clearly as I hear your voice with my ears. But it's rare for me to feel a link to anyone else." *You are an exception, but I think you're working very hard to get through to me.*

"There's more, isn't there?"

"I'm very intuitive. Extremely sensitive to mood, attitude, underlying agendas."

"Interesting," he said.

"Difficult." *Difficult to not acknowledge yours.*

"How?"

She chose her words carefully. "I often know what I shouldn't." *Like your desire to see me naked.* "Or forget others don't have the same edge."

He laughed. "Now *that* I can relate to." *And I'd best put up a shield before I get slapped.*

Sarah felt the change in energy, wondered about it. "I often have feelings I can't explain. Anything from foreboding to delight. Then I have to wait to find out why. Wait for things to unravel, so to speak."

"And you believe the feeling comes before the actual event and more frequently than accountable by coincidence?"

"Yes, exactly." She hesitated for a heartbeat, then plowed on. "And I believe this facility is connected to that kind of anomaly."

"We are devoted to the sciences of traditional medicine, alternative medicine, and psychic phenomenon such as mind control."

Her horror must have shown on her face because he held up his hand, and explained. "We work with people trying to gain control of their *own* minds. For example we can teach you to take your feelings of foreboding and develop them into something recognizable. Transform your gifts into manageable skills, to make them more useful than they are now. You can learn to monitor and fine-tune your own reception.

"But." His smile warmed. "The best work we do is in recovery. Helping to heal and give back minds such as Grace's which have been tampered with."

"And this place is *government*-owned?" she asked, wondering at the expenses of such a clandestine and complex operation.

"After a fashion."

"Are you under the umbrella of a particular agency?" asked Sarah.

"No. Etcetera does business with many different agencies and governments—all of which are

167

internationally protected. And because we often deal in areas most traditional scientists still have trouble with, we try to stay under the radar of the skeptics. There's no point trying to convince those with closed minds." He smiled. "*We* know the earth isn't flat—so to speak. And that's good enough for now."

"Well."

"Yes, well. Any questions for me?"

"Are you hiring?"

He laughed then, and his face suddenly looked quite different. Younger. "Seriously?"

She nodded.

"You just never know."

They went on to discuss Grace's relationship with Isaac and her mother, all information Grace had given Sarah permission to share.

The outline of Grace's treatment was the last subject on the agenda.

First and foremost, Kelton's team would work with her to recover all memories associated with Isaac's murder. Then the focus would shift to helping her work through her grief, the pain she'd never actually experienced because of the drug implants. Attempts would also be made to remove the programming, the suggestions planted in her subconscious by Dr. Kusavinski.

It would all take a great deal of time and patience, but hopefully, Grace could regain stability without the use of mind-altering drugs.

When the session was over, Sarah walked out of his office feeling hopeful about Grace's recovery, but something else niggled at her, and every now and then a picture of Dr. Kelton flitted through her mind. An interesting man, much younger than she'd first thought, and he had an incredible warmth about him. He genuinely cared about Grace. He wanted her to be well, to get her life back. And that, thought Sarah, must be the basis for how she was beginning to feel about him.

She was smiling when she went back to Grace's room and was pleased to find her sister dressed and waiting for her. They were being taken to a suite, the place within this massive underground facility they would call home for a while.

Sarah's own life had been put on hold, her patients handed over to a colleague, while she had "gone to Canada to nurse a sick relative." She'd thought the subterfuge quite amusing, but only because it had been so easy to do. One little lie and no one cared anymore where Sarah Rideout was. Or why. So much for importance.

Chapter 19

Six weeks later, Grace had a breakthrough. Regained complete recall of every memory she'd been previously stripped of. Remembered minute details of the night Isaac died. And she was furious with Dr. Kelton.

She'd gone back to the suite, told Sarah she needed some space, and spent the evening alone, stewing, fuming, wanting desperately to confront... But she was just as determined to wait, to deal *him* a measure of uncertainty.

She knew he watched her sessions on camera and would be aware of today's progress. But she also knew he'd been manipulating her through her sessions from the outset. Being micromanaged day after day allowed her to see the pattern of the intended route to the endgame.

Today, walking into the therapy room, she'd been primed to take the final step, to recover her memory of the night Isaac died. She'd expected the pain, and was anxious to get it over with. But nothing had prepared her for the revelation of Christopher Kelton's part in the nightmare she'd endured.

The shock had nearly jolted her out of her chair

and the anger almost undid her.

Coming out of hypnosis, she'd been one shallow breath away from losing control, storming into his office and ripping into him. But that's what he'd be expecting.

Instead, she'd make him wait, make him suffer just as she had. Absurd, she thought, he could never endure what she had. But, dammit, the man deserved to pay for what he'd done. How dare he sit behind his desk and placate her for weeks on end when, in reality, he'd been part of the horror.

#

It was ten in the morning when Grace stepped into his office, closed the door with a quiet click, and leaned back against it.

Keeping her expression as bland as the one he wore, she studied him, looking for a chink in his armor. The silence was weighty. The tension palpable.

She stared at him for endless minutes, waiting for the heavy layer of control she'd placed on herself when she'd woken up this morning, to melt away.

The fire began at her toes and worked its way up, slowly infusing her body with heat as it climbed. Her jaw clenched convulsively and her eyes glittered with malice before narrowing to blazing golden slits. Her chest heaved with pent-up anger, and when she allowed her voice to escape, it was low, controlled. And venomous.

"Doctor. Christopher. Kelton. Highly-respected, powerful, exceptionally gifted..." She drew a sharp breath. "How dare you sit there calm and smug and alive, *YouMotherFuckingBastard! You* left my father to *die*. *You saw* the blood pouring out of his chest, and you *left* us there alone. And why? So you could chase a fucking mugger? Isaac was *dying* in my arms and the best you could manage was, 'I'm sorry'? You're a doctor for God's sake! But you walked away. You left him to die. You left me to bleed. Both of us could have died while you took off to chase the fool. Have you ever wondered? Has it even crossed your mind, Christopher? Have you wondered what would have happened if you'd stopped, if Isaac may be alive today? No. You wouldn't even wonder. You just wanted to catch yourself a bad-guy." She was running out of steam, winding down, shook her head sadly. "And you didn't even get that right."

"Grace—"

She snarled, *"It is definitely not* your turn yet. I've got more to say to you."

He nodded, waited. She drew a long, slow breath.

"I've remembered it all. Everything. Earlier in the evening Isaac had warned me about you. Said you weren't what you appeared to be. Told me to guard my thoughts. You tried to charm me. You asked to see me again. But I could feel it. You were trying too hard. There was no real attraction. I could feel your calculation." When she saw his eyebrow tilt up ever so slightly, she added, "You weren't as slick as you thought. I knew the subtle flirtatious touches were no more than ridiculous attempts to connect with my mind."

"And what a mind it is."

"Shut up. *Shut the fuck, up!"* She longed to stomp her foot, but wouldn't give in to childish behavior.

"Who the hell do you think you are? Isaac said you wanted my mind. Well you can't *have* it. He said you were slick. And whatever you did or said was totally self-serving. And then," her voice chilled some more, "and then I saw it for myself when Isaac lay bleeding in my arms and you didn't even *try* to help us." She shook her head slowly, then her steely gaze locked onto his, and she asked with deadly quiet, "Were you in on it?"

"No."

"Why should I believe you? You let him die."

"He was already dead, Grace."

"No."

"Yes."

"You never even touched him. How could you know?" She loosened her fists, flexed her fingers.

"Grace, I have certain abilities. Please believe me. I knew his heart was beyond repair. Nothing could save him. He was as good as gone."

She stared at him, untrusting but suddenly uncertain. "Why were you there?"

"For Isaac. I was trying to recruit him."

"Why?"

"It had become obvious he had to be connecting telepathically with the people he was rescuing."

"And?"

"We wanted him to join Etcetera."

"Why?"

"Someone with his abilities is invaluable. He was already rescuing women from the human slave market and there were lots of other areas he could have made connections for us. Interpol was willing to share him with Etcetera."

"But he turned you down."

"Not flat. He'd said he would think about it, gave us a date."

"The night he was killed."

"He said he had something very personal to attend to and he'd give me an answer when the gala came to an end."

"Did he?"

"Grace, I'd like to tell you my version of the night he died, if you'd listen." When she shook her head, he held up both hands as though in surrender. "I believe Isaac would like you to hear this."

Nothing left to lose, she thought. "Fine. Go ahead."

"I was attending the function for two reasons. One, to talk to Isaac, and two, to do some telepathic spying on a couple of diplomats.

"I was standing at the edge of the dance floor, telling Isaac how impressed I was by the entertainment he'd provided, and he informed me all the dancers I'd seen so far were women rescued from human traffickers. It was the opening I'd hoped for. I told him more about our program and asked if he'd be interested in joining us. He began to answer me, saying the deal had been to talk after the gala, but then was suddenly distracted. Being an empath, I could feel his intense emotions, and I followed his gaze to see an incredibly graceful and elegant dancer coming across the room.

"You were in costume, a body suit matching your own skin color. You appeared to be naked. The crowd silenced as you made your way toward us.

"I asked, 'Who is she?' and he replied, 'The love

of my life. The reason I breathe.'"

Grace fought the emotion rising in her throat and sagged back against the door as he went on.

"I said, 'She's stunning, you're a lucky man.' And his reply was, 'Right now, she belongs to me, heart and soul. But in just a few minutes, in the center of the dance floor, she will discover her own wings, and I will set her free.' He looked at me then and said, 'You'll have your answer at midnight.' So I watched you dance with Isaac, and I saw him set you free."

Grace's heart fluttered, remembering. The floor, the room, the very air had been hers. Isaac had choreographed *Renaissance* for her, using Meredith's *Born to Dance*. And she *had* been reborn that night, freed from the horrors of the dance school, given permission to soar. There was nothing she couldn't do when the song ended, and she'd been elated.

She shook off the memories. "So he strung you along then snuck out at eleven-thirty."

"Something like that. I almost missed the two of you getting on the elevator. I ran down the stairs but came out the door too late. It was already over. Isaac's aura, his energy was gone, and I needed to know who the assailant was. There was nothing I could do for Isaac. I called for help while I chased the perp. I saw the car he got into, recognized the driver, and was pretty sure who the shooter was."

"You never went to the police."

"There was no point." His hesitation was brief, then just two quiet words. "Diplomatic immunity."

Grace straightened up, stood with feet planted, and hands fisted. "It was *murder*."

"I didn't see it. All I saw was a man getting into a

car very quickly. There was nothing I could do, Grace. You never saw his face, I never saw the crime."

"I *did* see his face. I know who he was and why he killed Isaac. I know everything."

"But I thought…" His brow furrowed. "You said otherwise."

Her smile was small and grim. "I have my memory back."

"You know who killed Isaac?"

"I know who put the bullet in his heart, who ordered his execution, and why."

"Tell me."

"You? The master manipulator? Not likely."

Kelton's face remained impassive. "What do you mean by that?"

She advanced toward him, stopped behind a winged-back chair, and propped her arms on it. "By some suspicious twist of fate, you have me and my mind here under your microscope." Her gaze narrowed. "I should tell you now, I don't believe in coincidence... Christopher."

"Ah, so you're thinking I sent Logan on a mission to get under your skin, break you down, and drag you in here."

"Exactly."

He threw back his head and laughed while Grace steamed silently.

When he finally sobered, he said, "Have you worked out all the details, Grace? Have you figured out exactly how we managed to pull it off? Did we pay Meredith to sing the song that tears you apart? Direct you onto the wrong elevator? Plant Logan in the parking garage so you'd run into him right in the middle of an unpleasant bust?"

She scowled while he continued, his voice softening, "I don't believe in coincidence either, Grace. But I *know* everything in this life happens for a reason, and I am convinced your connection with Logan was predestined just as you were meant to someday work with me. From the moment I met you and Isaac, I've known you would come here, somehow, sometime."

With just the right tone of sympathy he said, "I understand you're overwhelmed right now, but things will smooth out and you'll feel better in time."

Patronizing bastard. "Tell me honestly why Isaac refused to work with you before. Why he ducked you that night and why he wouldn't let you near me."

"Isaac was fully involved in his Interpol project. I believe he thought involvement with ETC would cause complications. He'd let us believe *he* was the telepath connecting to the women he was rescuing. Until the moment in the parking garage no one knew of your abilities. I'm sure he was concerned you'd be exploited."

"That's it? That was enough to make you back off?"

As Kelton stared into Grace's eyes she could feel the push of his mind's voice. *Isaac wanted to protect you, keep your power hidden. He was afraid because of what happened to the dance teacher. He had no proof but he thought you may have been connected to....*

Grace's expression didn't so much as flicker, but in her mind she created the loud slamming of a very heavy door.

Kelton smiled, nodded slightly as if to say, *Fine, we'll play it your way.* "When you asked to meet with me today, I anticipated the nature of our discussion and took the liberty of inviting a few people to join us."

"Observers, Kelton? This may be your turf, your lab, but this rat doesn't run mazes or do tricks so tell your 'few people' the show's over early." She moved around the chair, advanced on him, laid her palms on his desk, and ground out the words, "I'm fucking done here."

She spun to leave, but before she could reach the door it opened. Sarah and Dr. Kusavinski looked startled by the expression on Grace's face.

"What's wrong?" Sarah's voice was quiet.

"I'm leaving."

"I'll go back to the suite with you," she said.

"No. I'm done with this place and these freaks. I'm outta here."

"You can't. You're not ready."

"I don't recall being asked to become an experimental rat. I am *not* giving my mind over to science, and I *am* going home now."

"How?"

She heaved a sigh. "Sarah, the place has doors. I'm sure I can eventually find one leading out. I won't be held prisoner here any longer."

There was a hint of resignation in Kelton's voice. "You are free to leave, Grace. But when you agreed to Dr. Kusavinski's implant treatment you were well aware it was an experimental procedure, and you did consent to ongoing evaluation."

She wheeled around and snarled, "The implants

are gone, Kelton. And so am I." She marched out of the office, and his voice slipped softly into her mind.

Third door on the left.

It was labeled 'electrical'. She didn't even hesitate, wrenched it open and headed up two flights of stairs, where a car sat, with a driver, apparently waiting for her.

Chapter 20

Eight hours in a vacuum tube thousands of feet above the earth had left Grace groggy and disoriented. She deplaned amidst a crowd of sleepy travelers and glanced at her watch. Three a.m. New York time, but she was in Amsterdam so it was nine.

The pervasive scent of fresh coffee was a minor distraction as she searched for a ladies room and slipped inside.

She washed, combed her hair, then stepped into a stall, struggling to get her carry-on bag behind the door with her. She wrestled it open and took out what she needed.

Peeling off her long brown sweater and baggy pants, she was left wearing a tight white t-shirt, and long, slightly wrinkled pink shorts. She twisted her hair up into a knot and covered it with a pink ball-cap she'd doctored with a fringe of blonde hair. She toed out of her loafers, tugged off the warm socks, and slipped bare feet into pink sandals.

She pulled out a tiny mirror, and applied a quick dusting of pale powder, pink lip gloss, and blue contact lenses. She folded and slid the black carry-on bag into a beige canvas duffel.

Leaving the stall, she slung the bag over her shoulder, and strolled through the crush of women waiting at the doorway.

As expected, she was processed through customs quickly. She climbed into a cab less than an hour after touching down.

Grace ignored the exhaustion pulling at her, there was much to be done before she dared rest.

The taxi delivered her to a large American-style hotel. She checked in and went to her room. From the canvas duffel she pulled out the black carry-on, set it on the luggage stand, and opened it for her next disguise. This time Italian. She spent a little more time now doing the make-up, nails, and wig with great care.

Thirty minutes later, she left the hotel dressed in an elegant cream-colored dress. Her jacket, fine leather shoes, and oversized shoulder bag were just a shade darker, and an ebony wig accentuated the charcoal tint of her contacts.

She stepped into the daylight, nodded to the doorman and requested a taxi, her Dutch slightly affected by an Italian accent. Damn, but it felt good to be playing again. She nearly giggled.

Several changes of clothing, wigs, a plane, a train, and a bus later, she arrived in Zurich. There, dressed casually, looking like one of the locals, she slipped into a small but lovely apartment building, and stood holding her breath outside the door to number six.

Stomach clenched, and breath held, she lifted her hand to knock, but the door opened before she made contact. A tiny old woman stepped back, waiting in silence for Grace to enter.

The locks were set with care before the two women embraced and stood there, locked in their own emotions.

Katarina made the first move. She leaned back, looked up, and her smile widened as she stared into the same golden eyes her son had been born with. "Oh, Isaac," she breathed.

The pictures he'd sent of Grace over the years, at first a child, and then a woman, should have prepared her for the likeness to her son, but still, it was a jolt to an old soul.

Noticing the pain in her gnarled hands, she loosened her grip on Grace's fingers.

Grace stepped back. "I'd have known you anywhere. You have his smile."

"As do you, my dear."

"For many years Isaac led me to believe you were dead or I'd have come to you so much sooner. After we danced on that last night, he shared your secret. It was as though he knew."

"He did anticipate his demise. He didn't know the how and when, but told me he'd die violently, and soon."

Grace looked startled and her voice was barely a whisper. "He didn't tell me."

"He considered doing so, but decided it would taint whatever time he had left with you."

"How long? How long did he know?"

"Six weeks."

Grace closed her eyes, waited for her insides to settle. "That's why he pushed me to dance. Why he said it would set me free."

"He was determined to give you back your wings.

The ability to express what was in your soul. He vowed it would be his parting gift to you."

Grace's heart ached, her throat was thick with tears. "I wish—"

"He did the best he could for you and hoped you could go on without him."

Grace kept her eyes shut while she fought to regain her composure. She had a job to do. A promise to keep. She took some long deep breaths, and when she opened her eyes, Katarina was gone. Startled, she spun around, and saw the old woman, her grandmother, carrying a tray into the room.

Taking it from her, to place on the table between two overstuffed, brocade chairs, Grace said, "I wish I'd had a chance to know you sooner."

Katarina shook her head. "That wasn't possible. I had no choice but to disappear. I'm sorry, but it was a sacrifice I wouldn't hesitate to make again."

"I understand. Logan told me about your participation in his work. Our work. I've a promise to keep now, and I'm hoping to tap into your resources, your connections. I need your help."

The old woman pointed to the tray. "There is cream for your coffee, and please have a pastry."

#

Logan sat in Kelton's empty office and wondered what was about to happen. Would Grace be coming through the door? Was she okay now? Did she want to see him? Did he want to see her? It had been eight months since he'd walked away.

The door opened, then closed quietly behind the

doctor. He held out his hand, "Logan, good to see you. Thanks for coming."

"Being summoned by the head of an ETC department leaves little room for choice." He didn't appreciate the terse message he'd received shortly before midnight, *Be in Kelton's office at oh nine hundred tomorrow.* He'd just finished a job and had planned on a little down-time. And this renewed speculation about Grace added to his tension.

"I needed you for this assignment and there was little time for polite invitations." Kelton picked up a remote control and pointed at the screen on the wall behind Logan. "The answers to your burning questions are, yes, this is about Grace, and, yes, she was doing very well last I saw her which was several months ago." He slipped a disc the size of a penny into place. "Now this is one hell of a sensitive project so if you could just watch the video and save your questions, an explanation will follow."

They both turned their attention to the screen.

It was a children's dance recital. Thirty young girls, aged maybe six to thirteen, stood on the polished floor of a large stage. Ornate woodwork to the sides and heavy blood-red velvet curtains hanging behind them, the dancers, at first glance, appeared to be painfully thin, pale, and naked. But while their arms and legs were bare, their frail bodies were covered by thin, off-white, scoop-necked leotards.

The camera zoomed in on several faces and Logan's stomach soured at what he saw in their eyes. These were not a bunch of happy children nervously flitting across a stage. Their movements were stilted, their faces garish with makeup. Some eyes showed terror, others were glossy as the floor, with about as much expression.

The camera singled out one dancer.

Logan's breath sucked in as the realization struck. It was Grace at about ten years old, taller than the other girls, all legs and arms... and struggling. Her huge eyes swam with tears, and her cheeks sucked in as though she was biting the insides of them while she concentrated on the music and the steps.

The camera angle changed. Other girls came into view, then the entire stage, and, finally, cushioned seats covered with more red velvet. About forty men in the first two rows made up the entire audience. Logan saw one or two of them lean together as though to share a comment. Occasionally a hand lifted to point at one of the children on stage.

Dr. Kelton increased the volume so Logan could hear the music, the voice of Meredith, singing one of her most famous songs, *Born to Dance*.

Suddenly alone at center stage, Grace fought past the awkwardness of her gawky limbs, and struggled with intricate footwork. She stumbled twice but never quit, gritting her teeth and dancing on. The music stopped, and a tall man with a tidy gray beard walked up to her. His hand cupped her boney shoulder and slid down her body, caressing her childish frame. It lingered too long at the base of her spine. Slowly, he kissed her on both cheeks, then smiled at the camera.

Rage churned in Logan's gut. He forced himself to stay perfectly still and watch the remaining footage. Each girl had about a thirty second solo before the recording ended.

Logan rubbed his shaking hands over his face

while he attempted to digest what he thought he'd seen. It took a moment to find his voice. "Okay, Kelton, I understand why she was terrified of you with your beard, what's your point?"

"Oh, there are several points to make here, but first of all, I'd like to ask you this: do you think her mother saw it?"

"The tape or the man touching her?"

"We know she saw the tape. It was done by one of her staff. They had intended to use some of the footage in a video release of the song."

"But they didn't?"

"According to her, the artistic director said it was too bland, that the girls should have been wearing brighter colors."

"Have you talked to this person?"

"Yes, and he claims he only watched it once and thought the girls didn't do the song justice."

"Jesus. Why didn't anyone question what was going on?"

"Times were different then. Twenty years ago, there was little dialogue regarding child abuse."

"It makes me sick to know her mother and other people who knew her actually watched that and did nothing."

"Want to hear what happened next?"

"Probably not, but I'm sure you're going to tell me."

Kelton smiled. "It's a happy ending, Logan."

"Someone took out all the adults with a machete and the children were free to live happily ever after?"

"Not quite so wonderful, but the man with the beard *is* dead."

"And his damage lives on."

"Some of the men in the audience are also dead, but the children *were* rescued. Most have gone on to lead relatively normal lives."

"*Most*? What about the rest?"

"Two suicides, four dependent on alcohol or drugs."

"And then we come back to Grace."

"And Isaac."

Logan raised his eyebrows and waited.

"Isaac rescued Grace. Then, with help, he freed others."

"Who was the help? Please tell me it was official."

"Official... and Classified."

"So if I am to trust my inner voice, Isaac's death all those years later is connected to this."

"You are very rarely wrong, Logan, which is why I am constantly asking for an opportunity to work with you."

"Doc, we've gone over this before. I don't want to be part of your team. And my, ah, abilities are private."

"But we need them."

"What for?"

"To find another group of children just as endangered as the ones in this old video. You see, the puppeteer lives on."

Logan sat up. "Where?"

"Eastern Europe."

"Pretty vast area. You must have something more specific."

"I knew exactly where the operation was the day

Isaac died. But I don't know where it is currently."
Kelton hesitated for only a moment, leaned forward,
and said, "They are cultivating, culling, and selling
children. It has been going on for years. Isaac and
Grace had finally identified the man at the top and
were about to blow the whole thing out of the water.

"Now Grace is determined to carry on alone.
She's recovered her memory and her strength. She will
listen to no one and refuses to be stopped."

Logan half-smiled, half-grimaced. "No kidding."
Her tenacity didn't surprise him. But he couldn't
imagine her pulling off a mission like this alone.
"Can't Interpol work with her?"

"They could, and want to."

"But?"

Kelton knew there was about to be an explosion
in his office. It couldn't be stopped. He'd spent several
hours trying to think of a way to avoid it. In the end,
he'd figured it would be best to do it quickly, get it
over with, deal with the impact, then move on. He
sighed, closed his eyes, said a silent oath, and then
watched Logan absorb the words. "We can't find her."

Logan's internal words reverberated in Kelton's
head. *What? Like a fucking pair of gloves? You know
they are there somewhere, but you just can't seem to
put your hands on them?*

Words ground out between Logan's teeth. "You
mean to tell me this," he swung his arms wide, "this
department full of psychics, mind readers, mediums,
clairvoyants, intuitives, and God knows what else,
can't come up with one lousy lead on a simple mortal?
You've found kidnapped children, buried evidence,
missing pieces of every conceivable puzzle, and you

can't find one mere woman?"

"She walked out of here extremely pissed off. We kept her under surveillance for a long time until she slipped us. She's a free woman, Logan. We couldn't keep her locked up."

"Where's Sarah?"

"Right here." He picked up his phone, pushed a button, and said, "Now's a good time."

Logan studied Kelton, hated the grim resignation in his expression. Knew how bad this was. *Fuck.* He took a deep breath, concentrated, tried to keep the rage at bay, it would do no good. Information was what he needed.

Sarah slipped into the room, took a seat, and said quietly, "So how come the furniture isn't in tiny pieces yet?"

"Counterproductive," Logan growled.

"Please tell me you wanted to break something or slam your fist into someone."

Logan's smile didn't quite reach his eyes. "Oh, yeah."

"Good. Means you're still perfectly normal. Had me worried for a minute."

"Shrinking me, Doc?"

She squinted at him. "Just checking."

"So where'd she go?"

Sarah sighed. "She didn't share her plans with me."

"Come on, we both know you can read her thoughts."

Kelton interrupted. "Actually, one of the skills Grace learned before she left here was how to block access more effectively."

"Jesus, Kelton. Do you people ever think about what you're doing? Somebody like her, someone who can stop her own heart if she chooses, and you teach her even more control?"

"You'd rather we undermine her sanity? Make her *want* to check out? Take her power away? Even you don't believe she'd be better off imprisoned. The woman needed to be free, Logan."

"You're not making any goddamned sense, Doc. You turned her loose. Now, you bring me in, order me to find her." He pinned Sarah with a serious look. "This make any sense to you?"

"Ah..."

Kelton sat forward in his chair, leaned his arms on the desk, and said quietly, "I am not going to discuss the right or wrong of Grace's care. We have a serious problem here, and I am hoping you can help us. She regained her memory months ago. She knows the identity of Isaac's murderer and she claims to also know which high ranking diplomat ordered the hit.

"Bottom line, they know she knows, and given the opportunity, they won't hesitate to kill her. I have three different agencies trying to locate, her but *you* have the tools to find her."

"What tools?" Logan asked, his belly sick with fear for Grace.

"Your instincts. You understand her, and I think she trusts you."

Logan shook his head. "I'm not so sure."

Sarah leaned over and touched Logan's arm. "Way back when you first met her, you got through her armor. You affected her in spite of her defenses and she cared about you."

Logan grunted. "I wouldn't make book on that. There's little more than chemistry between us."

Kelton cut to the chase. "Are you saying you don't want to help find her?"

"No." He let out a frustrated sigh. "In fact I'm about to try the impossible and I have no idea why."

"You love a challenge."

Kelton smiled at Sarah, and passed a large manila envelope across the desk to Logan "This is everything we have so far. Read it, I'll be back in half an hour to answer your questions."

Chapter 21

Nancy slipped her hand into the biometric reader slot and waited. When the tiny green light appeared, she withdrew, and opened the front door to Grace's home. She stepped back and said to Logan. "I'll leave you here."

"Thanks."

"Do me a favor?" When he nodded, she went on. "Keep me in the loop. I know there are security issues, but I care about her."

"I'll do the best I can." He gave her a quick hug before she left, then closed and locked the door before trudging up three flights of stairs. Best to begin on the top floor, the most lived in area.

Grace's kitchen was what he'd expected. The cupboards were bare but for dishes and gadgetry like a toaster and mixers and stuff. The fridge contained nothing but a box of baking soda, the dishwasher likewise.

Furniture in all the rooms was draped with sheets. All the electronics, from stereo and TV to clock radios, were unplugged. On the top floor, in the master bathroom, the medicine chest held nothing stronger than ibuprofen.

He glanced outside and was again unsurprised. The pool had been drained and the deck cleared of everything, likely, he thought, stored in the padlocked garden shed.

Moving down to the second floor, he opened the first of three doors on the landing and recognized the dusty smell of disuse. He poked around what appeared to be a guest room and then moved on to Isaac's suite.

Photographs covered the walls and filled the shelves. Moving slowly from one to the next, he saw images of Grace laughing and playing as a teenager and as an adult, on horseback, on ice-skates, in cars, swimming, leaping high at a volleyball net, swinging a tennis racquet, and playing with her pets. There were very few of her dancing—those were always in a studio setting and always with Isaac.

Before Isaac's death, she'd been carefree, happy, and in love with life. Radiating confidence and sheer exuberance, reminding him of his favorite actresses from black and white movies. Yes, he thought, a young Katherine or Audrey Hepburn. A classic, strong woman. Until…

Logan shook off the punch of her presence, hell, she'd knocked him over before he'd seen how she used to be. But seeing these photos rocked him just a bit more than he was willing to deal with right now.

So he shut it down, went through the closet and drawers, looking for clues, and finding a treasure trove of memorabilia all tied to Isaac's mother. Everything from programs to newspaper clippings about Katarina, the world famous prima ballerina. The last clipping in the album, a tiny square of newsprint, her obituary. Isaac had been her sole survivor. Grace, who would have been eleven, wasn't mentioned.

Moving on, he took his search to the ground floor landing. One door led to the garage, the other was locked. He pulled a small folder from his pocket and spent several minutes fiddling with tiny tools. He heard a quiet click. When he opened the door, soft lights and music filled the cavernous room.

"Wow." The word slipped out as he took it in.

Not a stick of furniture. The floor was polished wood and the walls were... Well they were quite interesting—paneled with mirror and life-sized photographs of Katarina and Isaac, dancing. He strolled the circumference, took in the spotlighting, the speakers suspended from the ceiling, the built-in stereo system and control panel. He fingered the buttons and dials, noting the temperature, humidity, air movement, light, sound, and music selection could be done from one panel.

Behind the door he saw a cardboard-encased, flat package, about three feet wide and six feet long, with a delivery slip attached. He read the slip, noted the date and carefully removed the strips of tape. When he folded back the cardboard, he saw exactly what he'd expected, but it still took his breath away. It was another panel for the wall, a life-sized photograph of Grace dancing with Isaac.

It had been taken on the night he'd been murdered, mere hours before his life had ended in his daughter's arms. Logan studied the two pairs of golden eyes and saw love, strength, power, and vulnerability, all swirled together like the silken wisps of fabric floating from her fingertips.

Folding the cardboard back into place and

glancing one more time at the other photos, the smiling faces of Isaac and Katarina, he could feel Grace in this room.

As he left, pulling the door closed behind him, the lights went out, and the music stopped—in the middle of the song.

#

Sixteen hours later, he was in Amsterdam, the last place Grace had been seen and had one of her passports checked. He sat with an Interpol agent, watching security tapes, confirming it was Grace they saw deplaning, and finally spotting her, in disguise, walking out of the ladies room less than thirty minutes later.

"And that's it?"

"There has not been a sighting since."

Six weeks. She had landed in Amsterdam six weeks ago. She could be anywhere by now.

Logan stepped out of the airport and looked around, surprised by the daylight. He would have to find a hotel and get some sleep anyway. His body was thoroughly confused and his mind had gone to mush.

#

Logan traveled from city to city, country to country, watching and listening for something that would give him a clue. On the outskirts of Paris he'd spotted two little girls wearing tights and leotards who'd looked troubled, and he'd followed them, trying to hear their thoughts, discover what was worrying

195

them. It had taken nearly half an hour to get an answer. Turned out, they were walking to the hospital where their mother had been for several days. There was no connection to Grace or a dance school. And disappointment dogged him.

He spent his days on the streets, in squares, and markets. After dark, he sat at his computer, searching, scanning, for something, anything, while time marched on. And then, finally, a flicker of an idea. A direction.

The Summer Festival of Dance was about to begin in Budapest. And he felt sure, with so many dancers gathered in one place, he would pick up a thread leading him to Grace.

He updated Kelton, booked a room close to City Square, and grabbed a ride to the train station.

But two days after arriving, he found himself losing hope. He'd listened in on hundreds of conversations, talked to a few people himself, reached out telepathically, and watched for clues. There was nothing. Not even a hint of indiscretion.

Budapest was filled with highly-respected professional and amateur organizations and the visiting troupes, those just in the country for competition and performance, were carefully vetted. Legitimate dance schools had no connection to the slimy underworld operation Grace was trying to shut down.

So Logan gave himself a day off to regroup. He took a shot at forgetting his disappointment and recharging his batteries by visiting Hero's Square. He hoped the high-octane tourist energy and the historical depth of the place would serve to reenergize him, refill his empty coffers. He soaked in the rays of the summer sun while staring up at statues of men, and horses. Warriors, he thought. A different time and place, but what he and Grace tried to be. But he was failing. If he'd been in that older world, he'd liken how he felt to being unhorsed. On foot, alone, with miles stretched out before him.

The softness of someone else's thoughts slipped into his consciousness. *So sad.*

He couldn't resist the pull. *What's sad?*

That man. He looks quite forlorn.

Logan searched for the source of the thoughts, and found her to the north, in front of the Museum of Fine Arts. A girl of about sixteen glanced quickly down when he spotted her studying him.

Goodness, he's caught me staring.

Yes, I did, but there's no need to be afraid.

Her head came up in a flash, *You're him, and you hear me?*

He smiled. *Not many people in this place think in my language.*

I am American.

Me, too. Are you here to dance?

She laughed. *No.*

Could we talk?

We are talking.

I mean with mouth movement, sound.

Her chin lifted and she nodded at him. *Okay.*

Logan slowly made his way across the wide expanse to where the girl stood waiting for him. He held out his hand. "My name is Logan."

"I'm Jen, and I'm not used to talking to strangers." She made a sound rather like a muffled giggle. "With or without audio."

197

He stepped back just far enough to protect their personal space. "You sound American. Why are you in Hungary?"

"My twin sister is dancing here."

"But you don't dance?"

"Not like she does."

"Are you identical twins?"

"No. What are you doing here?" She studied his face. "Are you a dancer?"

He grinned. "No." He pointed to his shoes. "Two left feet and just the thought of wearing tights gives me hives."

Jen laughed out loud this time. "So why are you in Budapest, hanging out with the statues?"

His face grew serious. "I've lost someone."

"As in died or misplaced?"

"Misplaced isn't the word I'd use. She was supposed to be coming to a ballet school in Hungary but we've lost touch and can't seem to find her."

"There are many schools in this country. My sister has been invited to several of the best."

"And my niece has been turned down by all of them. I'm afraid she has more ambition than talent. A small private school finally accepted her. For a large sum of money, her parents were promised she would get the very best instruction. Private, individual coaching, what she needed to become a star."

Jen's brow furrowed. "Paying like that is not a smart thing to do."

Logan studied her suddenly serious young face. "How can extra training not be good?"

She heaved a sigh. "I have heard of bad places. The ones who take the leftovers."

"Leftovers?"

"The girls desperate to dance, but not talented enough to make the cut."

"Would she be in danger?"

"Parents tend to talk in a kind of code when they think kids are listening, so, I don't know for sure, but the tone was ominous."

"Then I really need to find her quickly. Could you help me?"

Jen actually felt bad for stringing him along, but she couldn't be certain they weren't being watched, listened to. She backed away from him, shaking her head. "I'm sorry, I can't."

"Why not?"

"I would be in a great deal of trouble. You see at the moment, I'm supposed to be somewhere I'm not, and when I'm discovered missing, well, it won't be good. I really must go now."

"May I walk with you?"

She looked at him as he settled into stride beside her. "I don't suppose I can stop you."

"Jen, am I making you uncomfortable or afraid?"

"No."

"Then I'll walk with you while you tell me where I might find my niece."

"There is a school one of the dancers talked about. She said it was in the mountains, in a village many miles from here. There are whispers about—" She stopped to look at Logan, and frowned. "About men."

"How old are you, Jen?"

"Sixteen," she lied.

"In the whispers, Jen, have you heard anything

about the girls being molested?"

"Yes, but nothing is actually said."

"I don't understand what you mean."

She met his gaze and whispered, "I hear their thoughts." Then she turned away from him to enter the hotel they stood in front of.

"Jen, wait."

"I really have to go."

"Could I talk to your mother?

"I don't have a mother."

"Oh. Well." He reached into his pocket for a card and wrote a number on the back before he handed it to her. "I'm staying right across the street. Call me if you think of anything that might help me locate my niece." He hesitated only an instant before adding, "But do not go sticking your neck out. Don't ask around or stir up anyone's interest about this questionable dance school."

"Are you asking me to keep a secret?"

"No, I just want you to be safe."

She nodded, and he studied her oddly. Perhaps something in her voice had poked at his subconscious.

Chapter 22

At ten o'clock the next morning, the cell phone in his pocket vibrated. Not recognizing the number, he waited until the caller left a message, then listened to the voice of his new friend.

"Logan, it was very odd. Someone else was asking about that school, just like you were. I will be in the lobby of my hotel for a while if you'd like to talk."

He called in first, let Kelton know he had a lead and he had a contact he was concerned about. Then he went to meet her.

As he walked through the door, he projected telepathically, *Jen, don't let on to seeing me. Try very hard to ignore me completely just in case we are being watched.* He spotted her near the gift shop, saw her sideways look, and smiled to himself.

'Hello, Logan. This feels quite strange, you know. I mean with someone besides my sister.'

'I don't want to make you uncomfortable. Why don't you sit over by the window so you can stare outside, look bored and still talk to me while I keep my distance.'

Without hesitation, she settled into an armchair

and got right to the point. *An old woman and man talked to me, asking about the same place you did. They said their granddaughter was there, but I didn't believe them.*

Why not?

The man was tall and looked old, but he was wearing some kind of makeup. And I think his beard was fake. The old woman seemed to be nervous.

What did you tell them?

I said I'd heard of a school quite far away in the mountains.

Logan walked to stand at the window on the other side of the lobby. He gazed out, not seeing the scenery, or even the people on the other side of the glass. *Jen, why did they pick you to talk to?*

I'm not sure.

Think about it for a minute, see if you can figure it out.

He waited, crossing his fingers in his pockets, hoping she could remember something useful.

As the girl mentally ran through the sequence of events, he caught a flicker of something familiar.

Jen. His inner voice was quiet, soothing. *Jen, think about the old couple for a minute. Try to remember details about how they looked, sounded, even moved. Roll it around in your head for a few minutes, okay?*

She complied and his heart nearly stopped. The old woman was Katarina, alive and well. And the old man? Grace, of course.

They'd probably chosen to speak to Jen because Grace had heard her thoughts just as Logan had. And there was a very good chance Grace had picked up a mental picture of Logan from Jen, just as he had of Grace.

Jen?

I'm trying, Logan.

You can stop now. You've done a fine job.

Did you figure it out? Why they talked to me?

He kept his face impassive while inside he smiled. *They were attracted to the openness of your mind, Jen.*

But I couldn't hear their thoughts.

They're very skilled at blocking.

I'd like to learn how. I mean how to.... to stop and start, I suppose.

Call me in a couple of years. I'll get you connected to the right people.

Logan, the old man told me I should never go to a mountain village called Solveik.

Logan smiled at Grace's blatant invitation, only a little surprised he hadn't picked it up from Jen's thoughts on his own. *Then you should certainly stay away. People rarely issue a warning without cause.*

Well, I have no reason to travel away from the city, so I won't be in any danger.

Glad to hear that. He thanked her for her help and promised to stay in touch, then made his way back to his hotel.

He put a call in to Kelton, and rather enjoyed waking the man up before five in the morning.

#

He left early and drove through miles of farmland interspersed with simple little towns. Tidy homes, functional yet decorative fences and concrete power poles lined clean streets. Once into the mountains, there was little to see until forest, dirt lanes, and guardrails eventually gave way to the town of Solveik.

Disappointment and relief warred within Logan as he drove through the pretty village. No waves of malice, no terror, silent screams, or suppressed fears greeted him. People didn't saunter the streets, yet neither did they scurry.

In clairaudient-scan mode, he experienced a normal range of reception. The presence of an unfamiliar car generated curiosity, yet no suspicion. The minds of the people he passed were not carefully guarded. Victims of abuse weren't being hidden within these well-kept houses. Children were not being groomed for market here.

He tamped down his frustration. Perhaps this was a starting point. There had to be a reason for Grace's message.

He'd wait in the tiny café. Choosing the table by the window, he ordered coffee and a sandwich. He watched a child tug at his mother's arm as they crossed the street. He nodded to the two elderly men at the back table sharing tobacco from a leather pouch. And he smiled at the waitress sneaking glances at him.

Then it happened.

A whisper floated across his thoughts, a single word suspended in a breath of air. *Brontosaurus*. His spine tingled, but he didn't so much as flinch. Only his eyes moved. His mind searched, called out, *Grace*.

He used the approaching waitress as an excuse to move his head, to innocently change his view. His gaze darted, found nothing.

With a deep sigh, he settled back in his chair and ate slowly, waited for Grace to call to him again, quite certain she would. But she didn't. He almost doubted he'd heard her at all.

He left the café, lazily wandered the length of the small town, poked around in the few shops, looked at souvenirs, bought a postcard and a beer stein. Back at his car he stood quietly, surveying the area, wondering where her voice could have come from, still straining to hear her.

He finally shrugged, got into the car, and started it. Or tried to. It was dead. Even the initial groan of the first attempt had faded into total silence. And then he heard her.

Tired yet Brontosaurus?

Where the hell are you?

If your car won't start, you should find a phone, call the rental company, a mechanic.

I have a cell phone in my pocket.

Better to ask a local citizen for the nearest garage.

Quit playing games.

Fine. I'm upstairs behind the green door. Pretend to knock on at least one other before you come here. The houses on both sides are empty.

He headed for the dwelling to the right, banged on the door, waited, then moved to the faded green panels of ancient wood.

One touch of his knuckles and it swung open. Once inside, he took the narrow stairs two at a time and there she was, standing in a tiny attic room near the window, smiling inside the face of an old man.

She chuckled at his expression. "Goodness, you

look surprised. Cat got your tongue, Logan?"

"Not yet," he muttered.

She stepped away from the window and he waited. She walked to where an old-fashioned black telephone sat on a small table, picked up the receiver, dialed a number, and handed it to him. "The garage. You need help with your car."

After he spoke to the attendant, she directed him further. "Go back out to wait for him. He'll tow it to the shop at the end of the street."

Logan stared into the golden eyes neatly obscured by dark gray contact lenses. "You have everything meticulously planned."

"I do."

"And you expect me to trust you?"

"Yes."

"Why should I?"

She huffed out a frustrated breath, "Look Logan, I need you to help me right now. Everything is settling into place and you're my ticket out of this village. I don't have time to explain right now, but I will soon. For now, just do as you're told okay?"

He wanted to grab her by the throat and see the cool façade drop. He wanted to see the woman under the makeup. He wanted—

"You owe me, lady."

"Yeah, so what?"

"So—"

The hefty rumble of a diesel engine interrupted them. Without another word, he strode down the stairs.

#

About three miles outside the village, Grace pulled herself up from the floorboards of the back seat. She'd spent her time crouched there removing the latex face mask and gray wig. Now, sitting in direct line with the rearview mirror, she shed the old man clothing, neatly rolled the white shirt, suit jacket and pants, and stuffed them into a canvas bag along with large manly shoes, hat, wig, the face, and gloves which had made her hands look like an old man's.

Grace slid a glance at him in the mirror and grinned. "What, you thought I'd be naked under all those clothes? Expected a strip tease?"

"Oh, you may not be naked, but you certainly got a rating on the strip tease scale." She looked pleased and he laughed. "Let me know when you're ready to sit up front and I'll pull over."

In answer, a nicely tanned, very long, naked leg slid between the seats, the toes pointed and foot arched as only a dancer's could. The second leg followed, and just as he caught a glimpse of drab olive green fabric, she thrust her body through the space.

Her long fingers tugged the baggy pant bottoms into place just below her knees and fastened a big ugly button at the cuff. The tank top, barely a shade lighter in color and several sizes larger than necessary, hung loose to her waist. She'd dropped a wig of shoulder length mousy brown hair on the console between them and bent to slip on a pair of dusty brown sandals.

She was bloody good at the disguise game. He grinned at her, then swore softly.

"What?"

"I damned near forgot I was mad at you."

"Why?"

Why had his anger slipped? Because she was so... Well, she was something else and she got to him at gut level. Why had he been mad at her? Ah, easier answer.

"Mad because you did a disappearing act, stirred up all kinds of speculation, have at least four different government agencies in several countries in an uproar, and don't seem to give a shit about the people who care about you."

"But—"

"Hey, I'm just getting warmed up here."

"Well then, cool off, Brontosaurus, and save the ranting for someone who cares. What I'm doing is more important than anything you could possibly be pissed-off about."

He kept his eyes on the road. "Every once in a while it would help if you noticed there are other people in the world besides yourself."

Grace experienced a familiar wash of shame. This was all wrong. She wanted to stomp her foot and tell him he had no right to make her feel bad about what she was doing. This mission would save children's lives. She couldn't let him make her doubt herself.

It was blessed unfortunate she had some kind of chemical attraction to him. She couldn't afford the connection.

She glanced at his profile and pushed down the feelings trying to be heard. Yeah, he was damned fine to look at, sure he had a great mouth and knew how to use it, but that wasn't what this job needed. It needed a cool head, a calculating brain, the willpower, strength, and single-mindedness to step over, wipe clean, eliminate.

Dammit to hell, she'd been wrong. She couldn't

afford to take Logan with her on this after all. He was a bad fit, far too distracting. She had to get away from him. Now. She set her jaw, sucked in a shallow breath, and straightened her back. Her voice dripped ice when she said, "Pull over."

"No." Let her sulk for a while, he thought, maybe she'd get it in the end, figure out he wasn't the enemy. The woman needed a damn good shaking up.

Deep in his own thoughts, he was caught completely off guard when her hand snaked over and plucked the keys from the ignition. Logan was forced to grip the steering wheel hard with both hands in order to wrestle the car to the side of the road. From the corner of his eye, he saw her reaching for the door handle, and he snarled, "Don't even think about it. You can't outrun me, and once I get my hands on you you'll wish you hadn't tried."

She sat back, dropped her hands in her lap, waited for the car to come to a complete stop. In a flash, she swung away from him, wrenched open the door with both hands, and got her feet on the ground before he grabbed her by the hair.

Now sprawled on her back, awkwardly half in and half out of the car, she gripped the door jam and hissed, "Let go."

"No. You let go. You let go of all the crap, and tell me what the fuck's going on. I've about had enough of your games, woman." He gave a quick jerk on the fistful of glossy hair. "Get back in here properly and talk to me, dammit."

"No."

Frustration drained out of him. Defeat was etched in his words. "Fine, then get the fuck out. Go. I can

209

probably catch a flight home tonight and good riddance to you. Have a nice walk. Hell, have a nice life." His hand dropped to the middle of her back and he shoved, making her scramble to save herself from landing on her ass in the gravel.

She took a couple of shaky steps away, then turned, planted her feet and stared at him, her face devoid of expression. "You want these?" She held out her clenched fist, opened her fingers, and the car keys dropped to her feet.

"I suppose that makes you feel better, doesn't it, knowing you're still completely in control."

"Actually, I feel a little foolish now." She bent to retrieve the keys, plunked herself back in the car, and glanced at him. "It is your fault, at least."

He let his head drop back against the seat and closed his eyes. He was tired of trying to anticipate where she'd go, what she'd do, and why. "Why, Grace? Why the hell is anything you think or feel my damned fault?"

Feeling her lean close, he opened his eyes to watch her slip the key into the ignition. With the twist of her wrist, the car started.

"How about this? If we make it back to the city without killing each other, I'll tell you everything," she said.

He'd already closed the door to his thoughts because he didn't trust her. She was staying with him now because they were in the middle of nowhere. Only a fool would think she'd keep her word and not bail out the minute they reached civilization.

Chapter 23

"No Grace, you will tell me now, while we drive, all about this self-directed mission you're on." Logan's words threaded through clenched teeth, but his attention never wavered from the narrow mountain road.

No doubt didn't trust her, she thought. And with good cause. She stifled a sigh, and resigned herself to giving him enough explanation to assuage his annoyance.

She slouched down in her seat, put her bare feet against the dashboard, and looped her arms around her shins. With her eyes closed and her voice as free of emotion as possible, she delivered a drastically condensed version.

"It all began when Isaac went to check on costumes for an upcoming show. He noticed a seamstress sneaking looks his way, so he said hello to her and the accent in her timid reply caught his attention. When he spoke to her in what he guessed was her mother tongue, he'd seen panic on her face. Backing off so he wouldn't frighten her further, he swore he'd find out why she was afraid of him.

"Doggedly determined, Isaac spent months

befriending Rosa, earning her trust, and in time, he learned about an underworld so alien and horrifying he vowed to find a way to stop the torture.

"Rosa had come to the States, believing she'd been recruited by a famous American dance company. As expected, her travel and documentation was all handled, and the red tape dealt with. But when she arrived in the States, her passport had not been returned to her. And there was no dance company.

"Instead, she was held prisoner in a secluded mansion with fifteen other girls from Eastern European countries.

"The dancing they did was for men in small rooms. The costumes they wore had little to do with ballet. They were sex slaves in a country where they were afraid to speak out for fear they'd be thrown in jail. They were told the horrors of immigration prisons where men and women were housed together, where fresh young bodies were bartered for, and ownership went to the most violent bidders."

Grace paused, dug into her bag for a bottle of water, and downed a half dozen swallows before continuing without glancing Logan's way.

"Within a year, Isaac, became a civilian contact for Interpol. As a well-known choreographer, he was able to slip inside several exclusive circles, and the movement toward shutting down a disgusting criminal operation began.

"The FBI handled the task of locating and releasing the existing slaves in the US. Interpol concentrated on the location and apprehension of international ring leaders. An elite group of private, special op soldiers actually intercepted shipments, scooping the girls as they arrived on American soil.

"Isaac also provided a safe haven. His properties, all very exclusive and spread throughout the continent, were used for housing, recuperation, and education of victims until they were ready for placement in either schools or colleges throughout the country or in legitimate jobs.

"Interpol still hasn't been able to shut down the smugglers—"

So Grace was going to, thought Logan. Dozens of words begged for release while he forced his fingers to loosen their iron grip on the steering wheel. He didn't want to say the wrong thing. If he pissed her off and she did get away from him, she'd never let him find her again. At the moment, she'd decided to trust him, at least a bit, so he needed to be careful not to undo their tentative connection.

He ran a hand through his hair. "If I ask you questions now, will you answer any of them?"

"Probably not. Have you talked to Nancy lately? How are Milo and Careless doing?"

So it was to be that way. He followed her lead, talked to her about her pets, about Nancy. He let her steer their conversation throughout the next hour or so of small talk while he puzzled over what her next move might be. Wondered why she'd decided to make contact—what she needed him for, exactly.

As they got closer to Budapest, Grace twisted her hair up into a knot, donned the wig, and Logan thought, yes, at a glance, she looked nondescript.

"What are you smiling about?" she asked.

"Do you have names for all your personalities?"

She grinned and nondescript flew out the

window. "Complete with passports from seven different countries."

"How the hell did you pull that off?"

"Isaac, and Interpol."

"You worked with him?"

"Our extensive travels were always scouting trips. My ability to hear the voices was how we found many of the girls and women before they left their own countries. I would hear the anticipation, the excitement, and the worry. Interpol did all the follow-up once I could point to an individual.

"In the beginning, Isaac and I hated when they weren't stopped before they made such a huge mistake, but we saw over the years, it was the right thing to do. Every girl I spoke to later admitted they'd have found another way if one avenue had been closed to them."

"So it was always dance schools?"

"Oh God no. They're just one of hundreds of schemes. Mostly, people will pay very good money to be smuggled into our country. Dance and education themes were employed to get full shipments of young women. Prime stock, so to speak." The flippant sounding statement was directly contradicted by the set of her jaw, the stiffness of her posture.

"And catching the criminals behind this? The kingpins?"

"That was wonderful. With the combination of our language skills and my ability to hear thoughts, Isaac and I were able to work our way right to the top, to get most of the men. The ones with the clean hands, spotless lives, and extravagant tastes."

"Were they prosecuted?"

"No."

Logan wished he could see her face, but she was looking out the side window. "What happened, Grace?" he asked softly.

"They disappeared." Her voice was flat.

"And had no replacements? No one took over the business?"

She shook her head. "It always continued. We could never find out who was behind it all. It had to be someone with great power."

And the pieces fell into place. He struggled to keep his tone light. "You finally figured it out, didn't you? That's why Isaac was murdered. And why your memory had to be tampered with."

She didn't respond, and he left her be, while he found a spot and parked alongside the hotel.

When he turned to look at her, she met his gaze directly, and even with the gray contacts in place, he could see the pain in her unfocused eyes. She looked brittle. Tough, yet fragile. He got out of the car and came around to her door. When he opened it, she didn't move, stayed frozen in place. He crouched beside her, stroked her fingers, and said her name softly.

He watched her come back from somewhere very far away, take a long deep breath, and exhale very slowly. Her glance met his, her eyes huge.

"Hi."

"Hi, yourself." Logan took her cold hand and pulled her from the car. He grabbed her bag and walked her into the hotel, up the stairs to his room, and through the door in silence.

When he finally let her go, she shivered. "Logan?"

He lifted an eyebrow. "Grace?"

"How can I be half afraid of you and still trust you?"

"Good question. What about me scares you?"

"Sometimes I feel like I have no power when you're around."

"Power?" It was hard to not ask for more than what she was volunteering.

She looked almost lost standing there in the middle of the room. "I'm a strong woman, yet right now, you're making me feel so damned weak," she said with yet another shiver.

He closed the space between them, wrapped her tightly in his arms, and backed her toward the bed. Sitting, he drew her onto his lap, tugged off the wig, released her hair, and combed his fingers through it.

"And you," he said, "make me feel far more than I should."

She lifted her face and he swore softly before lowering his mouth and gently teasing her lips. She was so soft, so exotic, and so damned vulnerable. "This isn't going to happen, Grace." The taste of her pulled at his gut.

"Why not?" Her voice was husky.

"Because the timing is all wrong." Jesus, he'd never have dreamed such a line. "We have too much work to do."

Grace unfolded from his lap, placed her hands on his shoulders, pushed him back on the bed, and followed him down, her mouth firmly fused to his. She seemed intent on taking what she needed, torturing his mouth while her hands unbuttoned his shirt to stroke fire into his flesh.

He resisted. He felt certain—by way of lying there, letting her taste and tantalize while he did nothing or at least little to participate—he'd been resisting, hadn't he?

But his lack of response didn't deter her, and there was little he could do but give in when the tank top vanished and her skin burned against his. She wanted and, dammit, so did he.

He rose up to meet her mouth, grab her hands, and still them. He was rewarded by her beautiful smile.

A chuckle rose from her throat as she said, "Did I hear you say uncle?"

In one quick move he reversed their positions and was staring down at her. "Not likely." His hands cuffed her wrists, held them against the pillow as his lips feathered across her jaw, down her throat and back up to take her mouth in a long hot kiss. Coming up for air, he smiled at her. "How about you?"

She swallowed, and he saw something odd and unsettling flit across her face as her muscles stiffened. He rolled, slowly, pulling her back over on top of him, his hands cupped her face and her eyes filled with tears.

Chapter 24

The sexual tension evaporated, and Grace wilted against him, slid to his side, hid her face against his neck, and wound an arm around his chest.

He gently stroked her back and waited, as always uncertain with her, unsure what would happen next.

She began to shudder against him as though silently sobbing. He locked his arms around her and held on, trying for a moment to gently work his thoughts into her mind but she had her mind shield locked down, impenetrable.

Long minutes later she stirred, sat up alongside him. She was physically stunning, with smooth golden skin, and her naked breasts barely hidden by long, sun streaked hair. He lifted his gaze to her face, and watched flatness slip over the glimpse of pain in her dry eyes.

"Grace?"

He caught a flicker of sadness, then nothing.

"What happened, Grace?"

She drew in a long deep breath, let it out slowly. "Memories. Ghosts. I'm sure you've got one or two yourself."

"Why?"

"The business creates ghosts, doesn't it, Logan?"

"What business?"

She pressed the heel of her hand to her temple. "Spies, agents, heroes. You guys, us, them." She reached for her shirt, slipped it over her head and handed him, his.

He tried to choose his words carefully, rolled questions around in his head, cursed himself for indecision and finally gave up saying simply, "I'm not the enemy, Grace."

"Don't I know it." She shook her head. "But I knew. Even before I laid eyes on you, I knew you were dangerous."

"How am I dangerous when all I'm trying to do is help you?"

She half smiled. "My life changed because I met you. My nice, uncomplicated life changed. The simple pleasures are gone. Hell, look at me, back in disguises, tramping all over the freaking world, listening in, ferreting out, lost in the hunt, not trusting anyone." She heaved a sigh. "And now I can't even trust myself." She went to the window, kept talking with her back to him. "I'd forgotten how afraid I could be. How exhilarated I could feel. How alive fear makes me."

She turned. Naked pain etched desperation in her tear-streaked face. "And I'd forgotten how excruciating, how crippling, loss is."

She had her arms hugged around her middle. She glared at him. "I *knew* about the implants, Logan. I knew why they were there, and I was okay with needing them. I went in for renewals every six months." Tears slid slowly down her cheeks. "Because

219

they let me forget."

He felt sucker punched. "But the headaches."

"Oh yeah, I had killer headaches instead, but Kusavinski set me up with drugs for those. The implants brought me peace. They spared me the pain that slices at my heart now, and it was a welcome tradeoff."

She fiddled with the bottom edge of her shirt. Ran her fingers back and forth along the edge. "Call me a coward, but it's true." There was something tragic in her grim smile. "Three times now, I've called him. Three times I've hung up before he answered. But each time it took a little longer, and soon, I *will* ask for the implants again."

"God no." Logan's voice was barely a whisper.

"Yes."

"I thought you wanted to save the girls currently—"

Grace struggled with the lump in her throat. "I will. First. I gave my word, and even if it kills me I *will* get them out of there. And I will finish—" She closed her eyes and fought back the sadness threatening to overwhelm her. "Then I want my life back. I want the peace and tranquility of the implants. I can live quietly at Paradise and be free of the memories, the fear, the pain, and the uncertainty."

"And you'll be half dead."

She opened her eyes but stared at the ugly picture on the wall. "Why do you say that?"

"Because you are a woman meant for passion."

"Sex isn't everything Logan. It's just a means to an end."

The laugh he choked back was pure reflex. "Not

sex, Grace. Passion. You have a soul full of passion needing to be expressed. You need to dance, to soar, to feel, or you'll never be free. Is it the proximity to freedom scaring you? Those ghosts, Grace—are you afraid of letting them go?"

She studied him while he walked toward her. His voice seemed to drop an entire octave. "You almost have your self back. You're clicking on all cylinders, your goal is in sight, and now you're what? Afraid of failing?"

She gritted her teeth. "I'm afraid of *not* failing. I'm afraid of the success, of wanting more, of an insatiable appetite for more. More of what will leave me empty and wanting. More of something that will cost me everything."

Now he did laugh. "Princess, we all want. It's normal and it's good. Complacency is for the aged and the dying. Hunger keeps us alive. Want and need drive the beast, Grace. There's no way around it if you're human."

She frowned at him. "Your argument is pretty good, but all you really want is sex."

Logan's heart gave an uncomfortable thump as he stepped in, framed her face with his hands. "Sex is good. Hell, I'm betting sex with you would probably be out of this world, but all of a sudden, I want a lot more from you. My hunger goes way deeper than sex, Grace."

He watched her digest his words, then kissed her with utter tenderness, and just before it led where he wanted to go, he stopped, lifted his mouth from hers. "I think we need some fresh air, a diversion." She didn't say a word. His thumb brushed her bottom lip.

"How about some tourist time, Grace? Just pretend for a couple of hours there's no other reason to be here but to see the sights."

She nodded, kissed him lightly, and picked up her canvas bag. She dumped the contents on the bed. "So, who should I be?"

Logan looked at the jumble of wigs and clothing, shook his head and said, "Surprise me." Then laughed at himself, grabbed her for a quick, hard kiss and muttered, "Again."

#

The afternoon and evening went by in a blur of innocent fun. They rode bright yellow trams, took a river boat tour, doubled on a scooter, walked for miles, took in historical buildings, famous artwork, amazing street theater, and finished up on the Danube Promenade.

"Ready to sit for a while?" Logan asked.

With one last glance at the beautiful Vigado Concert Hall, Grace took Logan's hand, as she had so often throughout the day, and replied, "I'm ready for food again."

He raised their hands to run his teeth across her knuckles. Heat spread up her arm, her heart did an odd double thump and her breath caught. She was so in trouble.

He led her to a patio alive with fairy lights, and they settled side-by-side to watch the colorful parade of tourists.

They ordered red wine *Froccs*, and a sampling of sweet delicacies off the pricey menu.

When the server delivered the spoils to their tiny table, she took a sip. "Who knew?" she said. "I've never liked wine spritzers, but give them a foreign name and serve them up with ambience, and I'm sold." She touched her glass to his. "To Budapest and days off."

His response was to hand feed her a morsel of dark chocolate dipped pastry. As she savored the sweet, she eyed the bit of chocolate on his thumb, and closed her eyes.

Chicken. His silent voice whispered.

She opened her eyes and focused on his. *We're out in public, for heaven's sake.*

You don't trust yourself to stop?

No. She glanced the plate. *I wonder if they'd package these to go?*

Logan laughed, grabbed her chin, and planted a hard kiss on her mouth. She put her hand to his chest to push him away, and instead, slipped her fingers up to his throat, grazed the warm skin, and heard the catch in his breath.

He pulled away, signaled the waiter, and they were soon headed for the hotel. He slung an arm across her shoulders, she carried the pastry box.

Tension built. When they arrived in his room, Grace pulled off the cheeky red wig, and kicked free of flip-flops the same purple as her shorts. The tightening muscles in her shoulders and neck prompted her to ask, "You got any booze in here, Logan?"

He came up behind her, sunk his fingertips into the tense muscles at the back of her neck, and worked the knots out as quickly as they formed. She let her head fall forward, and his strength seep through her.

His hands moved down her back, and he gently nudged her toward the bed. "Stretch out and let me do this properly."

"Logan."

"God hates a coward, Grace."

She laid face-down on the bed, turned away from him, and let the pleasure wash over her. He worked magic from the ends of her fingers to the tips of her toes. He kneaded, prodded, and pushed, massaging tension out of muscles until she was limp as overcooked cabbage, and unable to think… Then he pulled the comforter over her.

#

Logan woke first, watched her in the dim light of dawn, wanted her, but didn't dare to reach for her. Her face was peaceful and if he left now, there was a chance it would stay that way for a bit longer.

But when he came back less than thirty minutes later and spotted the empty bed, his heart caught for just the briefest second—until he heard the shower running.

Setting coffee and pastries on the small table, he shook his head, thinking, first I share a bed with her, hold her close all night without making a move. Now, knowing she's warm, slippery, wet, and naked, no more than twenty feet away, I don't even knock on the door.

He rubbed a hand over his face. Who'da thought? Jesus, what's next? Sainthood?

Logan was reading the morning paper, sipping coffee, when she emerged rubbing her wet hair with a towel and smelling like lemons.

"Morning, Grace. Sleep okay?"

"Obviously."

He set the paper aside and gestured at the table. "Coffee's hot, rolls are fresh from the bakery across the street."

When she reached for a pastry, he grabbed her hand, and with a quick tug pulled her into his lap. Her mouth opened to protest but he smothered her words with his lips. First devouring, branding her, then softening, to tempt, to fan the flame of her response.

Fighting for control, he broke away. She tucked her face into his throat and his arms kept her pressed against him while both of their hearts struggled to find an easy rhythm once again. When she finally raised her face, Logan pressed his lips against her forehead, then smiled and said, "Good morning, Grace."

"It certainly is." She winked. "But I have plans for the day," she said as she scooted from his lap to her own chair.

"I hope they include me." As in, *they'd better, because I'm not letting you out of my sight.*

"Have you ever driven a school bus?" she asked.

Chapter 25

"Not yet, but I suspect bus driving will be in my future," was Logan's response.

Grace nodded. "Second best answer. It'll do."

"Good. Now why don't you tell me why you're recruiting a school bus driver? The when, where, how. All of it. I'm a stickler for details. They come in handy when things start to unravel."

Her chin tilted up. "My plan is sound."

"Most are. But if other people are involved, things can change at any second without warning."

A groove appeared between her eyebrows and she pressed two fingertips against her temple. "We've located a school. I've had contact with some of the children—"

"We?"

She ignored the question. "They're all between six and twelve years old."

"How many total?"

"Seventeen."

"Okay, go on."

"They're being bussed into Budapest tomorrow to participate in auditions at a dance carnival. Or so they've been told. But I can't find any record of this group's participation. We're convinced it's a setup. I believe they're going to be sold, or shipped away."

"Can you be sure?"

She scowled. "Not absolutely, but it has all the earmarks of a sale."

"Tell me what makes you so certain."

"The girls have been training hard. They've been led to believe this upcoming audition could be their only hope for a future in dance." Her fists clenched in her lap. "One girl told me they have been teaching her how to be seductive."

"She said that?"

"Not in those words." Grace hesitated. "I had her go through it in her head, the dance, the steps, the attitude, nuances, gestures." She swallowed. "It was classic seduction. If she can move the way she has expressed, they'll have her lap dancing in mere hours." Her nostrils flared. "I *know* what they are doing to those children and I *know*—"

He laid a hand over hers. "I believe you. I just need to feel what I'm doing, to know as you do, why."

"Logan, you have no idea."

"Actually, I do." He held up one hand to stop her interruption while the other tightened on hers. "Kelton showed me the audition tape. Yours." He watched her face. "I can't change what happened to you, but I can save another child before they're sentenced to a life of servitude."

"Isaac saved me. What you saw on the tape was the end of it. I was not—He never—Isaac saved me before—"

"Yet twenty-some years later you were instantly terrified by the sight of a man with a gray beard leaning over you."

She closed her eyes, swallowed hard, turned her hand over to grip his, and nodded. "Yes."

"So you understand why I will be beside you, helping you rescue these children."

"Yes."

He tugged ever so gently on her hand, slowly urging her back to his lap, he pressed his lips to her forehead. "Tell me about the children."

She curled into him. "Aanna, is ten. Her mother left her at an orphanage when she was five, and she lived there until the Master took her to the school last year. He told her she was probably too old to become a prima ballerina but with hard work, extra training and longer hours than anyone else, there was a chance she'd be picked up by a major company as a corps dancer."

At Logan's questioning look she explained, "Like a background singer, a good career but without stardom or fame." He nodded and she continued.

"Aanna took classes, day in and day out for about six months, then the Master began to work with her in the evenings." She swallowed. "He promised to teach her to be graceful, fluid, supple." Grace's voice broke. "He would help her get in touch with the power of her body, her femininity, to feel like a woman, to please..."

Logan wanted to tell her to stop, wanted to hold her closer, and kiss away the horrors, but he felt frozen, not knowing how to comfort, what to do. So instead, he stayed still, very still, watching her face, letting her feel what she had to feel, find her way through it. And finally she continued.

"Aanna has good instincts, had a mother who

loved her when she was an infant. She will be okay.

"Maria is more fragile, she was dumped in the orphanage at birth and he's had her longer, since she was only four. She's nearly eight now and she's damaged. It may be too late for her to ever mend properly, to discover who she is. My greatest fear is for her."

She took a deep breath. "They are not normal children. They have all come from orphanages, from many countries, gathered as one gathers sticks for a fire. And some burn brighter than others, have more heat."

His kept his voice low and soothing, "Okay, Princess, how do we get them out of there?"

A smile spread slowly across her beautiful face and the golden lioness eyes glittered. "We're going to hijack their bus."

He smiled and tightened his arms around her. "I do like your style. Weapons?"

"Of course." She went still again, her voice dropping off to a whisper. "Logan, have you ever killed?"

He sucked in a breath and looked away for a beat or two. "Why do you ask?"

"I want to know."

He didn't hesitate. Should have, perhaps, but didn't. "Yes."

"Me, too."

He was shocked still. He'd known she had baggage. Had seen her as a victim. But would never have dreamed that she had killed. Her voice cut through his thoughts.

"Are you afraid of killing again, Logan?"

"No."

"I am."

"Why, Grace?"

"When I feel the terror of the children, the hatred and pain inside of them, it wells up in me, and I am afraid of it exploding. I am afraid if I see him I'll kill again. I am terrified I might react and create a link without thinking. I don't trust myself to stop even though I've changed so much since the last time. I have more control now, and yet, less."

He realized what she was trying to say. "You used your mind to kill someone."

"Technically, I convinced a man to kill himself."

"Was his death your goal?"

"No. I was only a child. I just wanted to stop what he was doing."

"What happened?"

She sighed. "I was ten. I knew a lot more about sex than I should have. Through my own eyes and those of the other girls, I'd seen him expose himself, make them stroke him, put their mouths on him. I watched him in classes, eyeing everyone, rubbing his hand on his crotch, his erection was exposed by the tights he wore, and at the end of class he'd keep one of the girls behind to give them extra coaching. It was never about dance." She began to prowl the room.

He hated asking the question, but felt it was necessary for her to get it out. "Did he rape them?"

"No. Years later I realized he'd kept their virginity technically intact, it made them worth more. But they were well-used otherwise."

"So what happened to him, Grace?"

"It was almost by accident really." She reached

for the coffee she hadn't touched earlier. Drank it down halfway and then continued. "In class one day, when he slipped his hand inside the front of his pants, I willed him to dig his nails in and hurt himself." She frowned. "The look on his face changed abruptly. But it wasn't what I expected. As a child I didn't understand, of course."

"That pain brought him pleasure."

She nodded. "But what I did understand was I had made him do something. So I started experimenting. Playing with his mind. Making him do things."

"Like what?"

She crossed to stand at the window. "Oh, little things at first. Choosing different music, changing steps in a dance, reaching for things, looking out a window, wearing odd clothing like unmatched socks and such. It was childish but hey, I was only ten."

"You tested your power."

"I made him ask to have my mother's camera man at the try-outs. I figured he'd be found out then, you know?"

"So what happened? What went wrong?"

"Natasha died. She'd been granted a private audition the night before tryouts." Grace's face reflected the horror she felt looking back at the memory. "She was crying, calling out to me to help her and I connected. Saw everything she saw, felt everything she felt. Told her she'd be okay but she wasn't Logan," she said. Her eyes dulled. "Monsieur told us she had been accepted by a famous New York dance company, had already gone, flown to her new home in America."

She shook her head sadly. "She was gone all right. Dead. Mutilated. Her body dumped God-knows-where. But I made a solemn promise to her spirit. He would pay. I couldn't undo what had happened to her, but I'd make sure no one else ever suffered at his hand. I'd make sure of it. And I did."

"I poured everything I had into mentally instructing him. They found him dead in his bathtub. He'd cut his penis off and bled to death."

Chapter 26

Logan shuddered.

Grace lifted her golden eyes to his. "I killed him with his own hands."

His voice was soft. "No doubt every rape victim's fantasy."

"And I wasn't even a victim."

"Oh yes you were."

She came back to her chair, sat, and drank down the cold coffee. "I'm afraid the hatred will control me and I'll do it again."

"Princess, nothing will ever control you."

"But the blocking I've learned, the shields I've created, what if they keep my own conscience at bay? What if everything I learned at Etcetera backfires? I want you to help me. Prevent me from losing control." She plucked a pastry from the paper basket, then put it back. "I need to let you past the shields, Logan. So maybe you can stop me."

He smiled with relief. "Then let me in, Grace, and I'll be there for you."

She shook her head. "That's the problem. They taught me how to put up the extra protection, but not how to let it down. Yesterday in the village, it took extraordinary effort to reach you. Like trying to run in waist deep water. What if I'm caught up and mentally disengage? Can you create a pathway?"

His arms ached to close around her. "Do you remember the first time I heard you?"

"I wanted your touch, and you wanted Nancy to go away."

"You were willing to trust me. You begged for my help."

She swallowed. "I guess it was instinct."

"Do you trust me now? Do you want to reenact that connection?"

Her gaze met his and he felt her power. She stood and went to the bed, lay on her stomach, and turned her face toward him. Her eyes were closed.

"Then think of nothing but my hands and your skin. Just relax and I promise we can make a connection happen. Then we'll shore it up to keep it open."

Grace had her doubts, but wanted badly for this to work. She listened while he crossed the room, closed the blinds, then poured a glass of water.

She opened one eye as he set it on the nightstand.

Beautiful hands. Long masculine fingers, so strong, gentle, soothing. Touch me. I wish they would touch me.

Oh such an invitation and to think you don't really mean it.

Pleasure at the warmth accompanying him as he slipped into her mind made her smile, she rolled onto her back, looked into his eyes. *But I do mean it. Please touch me, Logan.*

He sat beside her on the bed, his fingertips lightly

brushed her forehead. *Be careful what you wish for, Grace.*

What was it you said before? God hates a coward?

Tart. His smile widened as she hooked her hands around the back of his neck and pulled him down to her. *Please tell me I'm not destined for another cold shower.*

"I hate cold water," she murmured against his mouth. "I will only shower with you if the water is very, very, warm."

"You feel like a shower?" he teased.

Her voice went smoky, "Maybe after."

"After?"

"Jesus, Logan, how much invitation do you need? I thought you wanted me naked."

His grin was just a bit wicked. "Only if I am, too." He pulled his shirt up over his head and as he tossed it aside, he reversed their positions so she was on top. He would be careful with her. Straddling his hips, she rose to her knees, and kept her eyes on his while she unbuttoned her blouse, let it fall away.

Drop-dead-fucking-gorgeous.

She threw back her head and laughed. *Not bad yourself, Brontosaurus.* Her mouth met his and the fire consumed her.

#

Grace and Logan slipped into the safe house at six o'clock in the evening. It was quiet.

"I thought we were meeting your team here." She'd initially resisted when he wanted to involve other people. But he'd been adamant, insisting the only way to pull off a successful recovery was by utilizing the resources available to them through ETC.

"When I spoke with Kelton this morning, he said the team would be assembled by midnight. Some were already on the ground in the area. Several others are probably asleep upstairs, trying to recover from their travels. And the rest will be arriving soon."

"Arriving from?"

"He drew from a worldwide collection to make up the best extraction team available."

"It's still my project, Logan."

Dr. Kelton walked into the room, his voice was low and serious. "But you can't pull it off alone, Grace. You need all of us just in case. The children need *us*." He glanced over his shoulder, reached a hand out behind him, and Sarah stepped from the shadows. He dropped an arm across her shoulders.

She leaned into him and smiled as she finished his sentence. "Because we're the best there is."

Grace stood frozen in the moment. She hadn't felt Sarah's presence. And the obvious intimacy between the two standing before her was a shock.

Logan pushed gently against the small of her back, and after a heartbeat of stillness, the women moved into each other, wrapped up and held on.

In silent agreement, the two men went to the kitchen where Brad and Cheryl were waiting. Logan threw a playful headlock on Brad, then leaned over with a grin and planted a noisy kiss on Cheryl's mouth.

"Hey. Get your own woman," grumbled Brad

"I did."

"Well then, keep your lips off mine."

"Aw, come on. You know she loved me first. Just felt sorry for you because of a lousy flesh wound. You mighta sucked her into marriage but it's my body she really wants." They all laughed at the old joke.

Years ago, Cheryl had been in Logan's living room, waiting desperately for news of Brad. He'd been out on a mission and disappeared after a nasty encounter with a terrorist group. When Logan broke the news that their recon-team could find no sign of him, Cheryl collapsed into his arms in tears. Moments later, Brad himself came through the back door, his clothing soaked in blood. When she'd seen him, she screamed, and fainted dead away.

Brad's response to the scene had been a muttered, "Nice try, pal, but she's mine." Then he'd slithered to the floor, unconscious. Brad and Cheryl were married less than a week later with Logan as their best man.

Another couple walked into the kitchen and Logan's eyebrows went up. He silently greeted the young woman. *Sneaky. I should have known you were a plant. Just too damned convenient.*

Jen grinned at him, *Worked, didn't it? Got you two together, didn't I?*

I feel so used. Then he chuckled, looked at Kennedy Williams, and said, "Cradle robber."

"Hey, not so. She's legal."

Jen spoke up. "And he's keeping his hands to himself because he's afraid of my husband."

Logan shook his head. "Gotta ask, how old are you?"

"Twenty-seven," She said with a grin. "Jake and I've been married four years. Ken was our best man."

"Kennedy Williams in a suit?" Logan laughed. "Hard to imagine."

"Hey, I can dress if I have to. Especially if it's on a dare." He winked at Jen.

Logan wasn't about to be sidetracked. "And where exactly do you fit on this team?"

Williams shrugged. "Had nothing on my plate so Jake asked me to travel with Jen. Besides, things go south, I could be useful."

Kelton stepped in with explanations. "Jen's married to Dr. Jake Brown. He loaned us his wife for this project because she's been doing a lot of work with abused children and has a great deal of success communicating with them. However, I had to promise she wouldn't be involved before they're ready for transport. Until then, she's just eyes and ears on this mission. Observation and telepathic connection. No hands-on stuff."

"Kids talk to me, trust me for some reason," she said. "But just so you know, I was in a special shadow program. I did ten months side-by-side with navy S.E.A.L. trainees, then went on to shadow green beret recruits for another ten months. The powers above had hoped to put together data regarding the unsuitability of females in those programs." She grinned. "I screwed up their stats."

"And her father heads up the American base for ICS," Kennedy added.

"Impressive," Grace said from the doorway.

Jen shook her head. "Not trying to be. I just want everyone to understand I'm not excess baggage. You need me and I'm more than capable."

Kennedy spoke sardonically, "Right, and just

remember, anything happens to her, my balls are on the line."

Jen chuckled. "Don't worry, I can handle Jake. Your precious jewels will be safe."

"And on that note," said Kelton, "we have protection signed on from several fronts." He glanced at his watch. "They should be waiting for us downstairs."

#

In a large conference room below the house, the four couples met the security portion of their team. The dozen men and women were an interesting mix of Interpol, FBI, IIF—International Intelligence Facility—and ICS—International Code Safe, an elite company of mercenary soldiers.

The briefing lasted six hours. The first three were dedicated to Grace's original plan—bumped up somewhat to include more team members. The last three were dedicated to alternative action, just in case things went wrong. They were completely prepared to scramble if necessary.

Chapter 27

"Why don't you sit down and talk to me about whatever's got you chewing the insides of your cheeks raw," Logan said.

Grace was momentarily startled by the understanding in his eyes. How much did he know? Should she have told him about Katarina? Or—? She tried to smile but failed.

"It will all work out, you know. We'll get those kids away from there."

She nodded and perched on the edge of the bed.

"Then why are you so worried?"

"I just hate waiting, dammit. It feels like I'm wasting time twiddling my thumbs."

"Then talk to me. Tell me about the first time you met Isaac. Did you know about him already? Or did he just waltz in and say, 'Hi, I'm your Dad?'"

She blinked, and something like a half-laugh escaped her throat. "None of the above. It's a long story, really."

"We've got hours, Grace. Tell me."

"Well," she said, "it was my first encounter with what some may call fate, or destiny, I suppose. In any case, it was a power-packed few days for a ten-year-old. A series of events to leave a life-long impression on my mind." She pushed back to sit cross-legged on the bed.

"I was tied in knots all week, anticipating the try-outs. It wasn't like anyone expected me to be chosen. I'd only been at the school a few months and even Monsieur said my height alone would probably mean a disqualification. But he drilled me for days, pointing out every flaw and weakness in my performance. I'd go to class determined to master the steps, but leave in tears, feeling hopeless and clumsy.

"I've already told you about Natasha, the girl who died the night before try-outs, and my connection to her. Well, when I felt her pain and her death, I went a little crazy. I fell apart, crying, and yelling at Meredith. I told her I wouldn't go to try-outs. I'd never dance again. I hated her song because it was obvious I *wasn't* born to dance. I was such a pathetic mess she resorted to bribery. Promised to take me to see Katarina, the world famous prima ballerina. And all I had to do was go to the try-outs.

"I worshiped Katarina. I'd do anything to watch her dance." Grace made a face. "I was ten.

"So, Friday I went to the big old theater with the rest of the girls, danced to Meredith's music, was photographed, videotaped, and interviewed." Her gaze met Logan's. "And I struggled to shut out the visions shadowing my mind. Thoughts belonging to the men in the audience, their plans, their fantasies, and their urges were nearly more than I could deal with. Men's big hands touching and shoving in ways I'd never seen before, but instinctively knew were wrong. What they imagined the girls doing, things I'd only ever heard about in whispers. With sickening clarity I knew many of the chosen girls would likely never dance again." She shuddered at the memories.

"When I got home, I couldn't eat without throwing up. Meredith thought I was overreacting to not being chosen."

"You were afraid to tell." It wasn't a question. He leaned back in the chair as though relaxed but she could see tension in the set of his shoulders.

"It didn't occur to me. You have to realize, I was growing up in a weird world of seeing and hearing what was in people's minds. With no one to tell me what was real, make-believe, deviant, or normal, I had no choice but to believe whatever I was exposed to was acceptable."

She ignored what she suspected was pity in Logan's expression. "Anyway, I was so freaked out, Meredith gave up trying to tell me there'd be other try-outs. She called the hotel doctor and had me sedated." She sucked in a huge breath and exhaled slowly.

"The next day Meredith fussed over me—which was unusual behavior for her. We went shopping for new dresses, spent the afternoon having our hair done, ate dinner at a fancy restaurant, then took a limousine to the Ballet."

Grace couldn't help but smile when she said, "Katarina was everything I'd expected. Amazing, beautiful, elegant, serene, and so incredibly graceful. I was mesmerized. She made me forget the ugliness. I cried while she took her bows, lost count of how many times the curtain went up." Tears welled. "She never danced on stage again." Grace shook her head and blinked to clear her vision.

"I went home with a souvenir program to cherish. The first ten pages were photos of Katarina, but there was also a picture of a tall, lanky man with golden eyes and a big smile. Her son, Isaac. The program said he'd been her choreographer for the last five years. I remember staring at the photo because he looked no more like Katarina than I do Meredith." She scooted back on the bed to prop herself against the headboard.

"Did you have any inkling, feel any sort of recognition?" he asked, steepling his hands in front of him.

She shrugged. "I don't think so. But on Sunday morning, a picture of us attending the Ballet made the local paper. Someone had done their homework and written a little story about the famous Meredith's talented daughter representing Monsieur's celebrated dance school at the national try-outs. That's when Isaac discovered he had a daughter."

"Did he contact you?"

Grace took a deep breath. "Yes. Tuesday, I had to go back to the studio, to class. I didn't want to go. But when I stepped off the elevator in the hotel lobby, a strange but comfortable feeling wrapped around me like a warm blanket. The pressure in my head eased, lightened, and I felt a smile inside. A man walked toward me. Isaac. Katarina's son. He said my name. He asked me to sit down and talk."

"Bold of him, to approach a child that way."

"I was giddy with excitement. I told him I recognized him from the pictures in my program. We chatted about dance for a while before he dropped the bombshell. My classes had been cancelled because the Monsieur had been found dead in his apartment."

Grace shook her head. "I was stunned by the news and horrified by the grin I couldn't stop. I wouldn't have to convince Meredith to let me quit dance.

"It was years before I wondered at a stranger, an adult, telling a child such news. But at the time it was only a relief. Isaac asked me to call my mother, but instead I took him to her."

"How'd that go over?"

She shook her head. "If you could have seen Meredith's face when I walked onto her set, hand-in-hand with Isaac, my new best friend. I, of course, had no idea he was my father. I just knew he was a famous choreographer and the son of Katarina. Poor Meredith. She asked someone to watch me, and dragged Isaac off somewhere to talk to him."

Logan waited but she didn't continue so he asked, "Did they tell you Isaac was your father?"

"Not then. Just that he was an old friend of my mother's."

"But he was part of your life afterwards?"

Grace frowned. "No. Not until I turned eighteen. Another long story—for a different day." She yawned, slouched down and settled into the pillows.

She'd nearly drifted off when Logan's cell phone signaled an incoming call.

"Yes?" he answered. "Hang on." He glanced over at Grace. "Jen wants to talk to you."

She reached a hand for the phone, but he shook his head. "In person. She's in the lobby."

"Sure. Tell her to come up."

#

Jen came through the door like a fresh breath of air, while Williams stood at the threshold, shuffling his feet.

"You take this guard dog thing seriously," Logan said to him.

"Never had this kind of assignment before."

"I think she'll be safe here with Grace. Why don't you and I go grab coffee while they talk about kids?" He glanced at Jen and asked, "That *is* why you're here, right?"

"Yeah. I thought I'd pick Grace's brain for a while so I'd have a good feel for the girls when I meet them."

Logan elbowed Williams. "Come on, pal. I know this nice little spot just around the corner. They've got great pastries, too." He gave the women a mock salute. "Later, then."

#

Grace smiled at Jen. "So what do you want to know about the girls?"

"Everything. Tell me whatever facts you have about each kid plus your impressions of their strengths and weaknesses. We need to establish which ones I can depend on to look after the others, if necessary. Who's most likely to fall apart or be difficult. We need to be prepared for the unexpected. We need our own plan."

#

When Logan and Williams returned nearly two

hours later, Grace was asleep.

Jen, sitting by the window, put a finger to her lips, and Logan raised his eyebrows in question. She pointed to the door and followed him out.

Once the door closed behind her, he asked, "What happened?"

"Nothing. She told me all she could about the children, then dosed off."

He frowned. "Not like her."

She smiled. "Nose outta joint because she trusted me?"

"You didn't drug her to read her mind?"

She gaped. "Of course not."

"Sorry."

She patted his shoulder. "I'd never do anything to hurt her Logan. She's been through too much."

His eyebrows shot up.

"Jesus, Logan, I didn't come into this blind. I've read her whole file, okay?"

"Yeah, sorry again."

"Go." She tipped her head toward the door. "Stretch out with her and get some sleep. You'll be less paranoid if you allow your mind to rest for a while."

"Hey, I may be a little suspicious, but never paranoid."

She tipped her head. "You sure about that?"

Chapter 28

It was finally time.

Two couples made their way into the hills on motor scooters to set up on the quiet country road where the school bus would have to travel. Brad and Cheryl were east of the old farm where the dance school was located, Grace and Logan were west.

Interpol agents masquerading as highway flag-men were positioned a mile from each so once the bus drove off the dirt track and onto the road, any traffic would be stopped and kept safely out of the way.

When an agent hidden in bushes at the entrance to the farm announced the bus had headed west, everything went quickly into motion.

Brad and Cheryl headed west. Logan positioned himself and the scooter in the middle of the pavement. Grace knelt over him.

As the bus rounded the corner, Grace jumped to her feet and ran towards it, stumbling, waving, and shouting.

The vehicle ground to a halt, and the door opened.

Appearing anxious, and bloodied, Grace scooted up the steps and pleaded with the skinny driver for help. She pulled him with her, off the bus, and over to where Logan lay moaning in the middle of the road.

An agent slipped from his hiding place among the trees to assist Logan and they made short work of taking the man into custody. Handcuffed and hogtied, they bundled him back onto the bus, loaded the scooter as well, and climbed in themselves. The entire operation lasted less than six minutes.

But something was wrong. Grace scanned the interior, trying not to look into the eyes of the silent girls. Couldn't allow herself to be sucked into their collective fear.

Maria? She waited. *Maria it's Grace. We've come to help you.*

There was a quiet gulp just before Grace caught the shudder running through a small girl four rows down. Their eyes met and tears poured from the child.

Aanna it's okay now. You'll be safe now.

Noooo, it's too late. Maria.... Even in the thought there was pain.

Aanna. Grace felt the blow to her solar plexus. *What's wrong with Maria?* she demanded. *Where is she?* Her gaze sharpened and scanned for eyes she thought she'd know. But saw nothing. Nothing but...

Where?

She... She didn't come with us. He said she was too ill. She'd ride in the car with him instead.

"Grace, what's wrong?"

She spun around to see Logan standing behind her, the bus driver bound and gagged on the floor at his feet.

There was no decision to make. She had no choice. Had a duty. "Let's get out of here."

Logan nodded and slid into the driver's seat.

Once underway, Grace dug out her cell phone, punched a button. "I need you now."

Within minutes Jen, on a scooter, came alongside the bus and signaled for them to pull over.

Logan eased to a stop, opened the door and Jen jumped into the bus as quickly as Grace jumped out. She opened her mind for the briefest of moments. *I'm sorry, Logan.*

Grace. What the hell?

Jen squeezed his shoulder. "Best get this crate moving, Logan. We have to get these kids out of here. She'll catch up later."

#

Grace searched nearly every inch of the farm. The biggest building, an old red barn, housed the dance studio complete with a mirrored wall, and ballet barre. Looking into what had once been three chicken coops, she saw mattresses on the floors and rickety bunk beds built onto the walls. The only apparent bathroom facility was an outhouse. The garage had been closed in, converted to a sort of dining hall, with three long tables draped in plastic with rough wooden benches alongside.

Inside the house, living conditions were far more appealing. Three bedrooms, a living room, and a kitchen were filled with fine antique furniture. The bathroom had a large oval tub. Grace stood frozen, with her senses screaming at her.

Terror, pain, and consuming darkness threatened to incapacitate her while a familiar metallic odor pressured her gag reflex. She reached for a white towel hanging by the sink, leaned over, wiped the soft terrycloth over the beige porcelain, then slowly turned it to see the traces of blood she knew would be there. Faint, but unmistakable. The tub had been rinsed, but not washed.

She closed her eyes, opened the channels of her mind as wide as she could, and called to the missing child.

Maria, she tried several languages and then just a steady singsong soft repetition of the child's name. *Maria, Maria, Maria....* but she heard no answer, felt no presence. She wanted to scream. Wanted to rail at someone, run frantically from room to room searching, but she knew the child wasn't there. Anywhere. Maria was dead, of that she was certain, but she fought the knowledge.

Her cell phone vibrated in her pocket. She knew it was Logan, needed to hear his voice, but couldn't let him inside her head. Not yet. She checked her watch. She'd been out of touch for an hour. Had to allow contact. She took a long steadying breath, pushed the talk button and spoke quickly, before he could. "She's dead. And she's not here."

"He had her in the limousine," was his curt reply.

"I have to go now. I don't know—" Her voice caught in her throat.

"What don't you know, Grace?"

"If I'll be able to do it, then live with myself after." Odd, she thought, I just felt a chill run up Logan's spine.

Tension poured through his voice. "Where are you?"

"At the farm. The dance school." She struggled to sound calm, detached. "Her blood's in the tub. She was dead before she left here. Where is he?"

"Dead, the limo went off a cliff, went to the bottom of a ravine and burst into flames."

Silence.

"Grace?"

She was struggling to breathe past the fury crawling up her throat. "Are you sure it was him, you're positive he's dead?"

"The team found three bodies, thrown out of the car when it hit bottom. He's positively ID'd, the child is probably Maria. The third is an unidentified man. They also found an elderly woman still on the roadway."

A horrendous pressure on her chest sucked the air from her lungs as knowledge and pain ravaged her body, and her knees gave out. She landed awkwardly on the side of the tub. Her mouth opened in a soundless scream as she clutched at the porcelain, and finally slid to the floor.

"Grace?"

Oh God, Katarina, no. She squeezed her eyes shut.

His voice was sharp, "Grace."

She mentally gathered herself, separated from her feelings, grew frozen inside. "Logan." Deadpan. Empty. All wrong, but she couldn't help it.

"Talk to me Grace."

It was a whisper. "Sorry Brontosaurus, I just can't right now." She pushed the off-button and said softly, "I am so very sorry, I just can't do that right now."

#

Logan had to continue driving the bus. He wanted to turn around, get to her, but sixteen young lives were depending on him. He glanced at the mirror, and Jen was there, nodding to him. *She'll be okay, Logan. Williams is watching out for her.*

What?

She has more to do. And you can't help her. She's going after the man who murdered her father.

Fury washed over him. *I fucking hate being used.*

You weren't. She was.

I want to know... everything.

Jen shot a glance over her shoulder at the wide eyes and pale faces of the frightened little girls. *Not now. They need me, and they need you to get them to the airstrip.*

#

Hours passed. The children were given warm clothing and a hot meal before boarding a military aircraft. Logan tried to get out of going with them, but he'd been given a direct order and had to comply. Jen, Brad, Cheryl, Kelton, and Sarah were also on the flight, destined for an air force base in Germany. There, the children would be checked out and tended before flying to their final destination.

Jen spent long tiring hours with the kids, often dragging Logan along with her. The girls needed to know men who were good and trustworthy. They needed to begin to understand that what had happened to them wasn't right. Wasn't normal. And, most of all, wasn't their fault.

Once the political red-tape was dealt with, the orphaned girls would travel to the States. They'd be first housed and rehabilitated at Paradise, then placed, very, very, carefully in loving homes only if and when they were ready. Logan was betting most would opt to stay at Paradise.

A few began to recover right away, others found it hard to trust anyone. And watching them, being around them, Logan understood more about Grace. He finally got it. She hadn't been abused as a child, yet she'd experienced abuse. She'd suffered through her telepathic and empathetic connections, so her damage had been exponential. No small wonder she'd been driven to save these girls.

But what now?

Jen had filled him in on the second half of Grace's mission. She was going after Alaxandar Malakorgov, king of the tiny country of Korgov. He was the one. The man behind all the child-marketing rings. The man so politically high up he'd been unreachable. The man who had raped Katarina and fathered Isaac.

Up until now, when an operation had been busted, someone on a lower rung had always taken the fall. Then, in time, he'd set up a new place in a different country, recruit new minions, find more children to exploit. He had the power. He had the glory. And he thought he was God.

Grace knew he wasn't. And she was determined to make sure he found out the hard way. Isaac had stood beside this man once and called him father. Grace would have to live with that. She'd have to live with assassinating her own grandfather. A man responsible for the murder of his son. A man so smooth the evil under his skin was invisible.

Chapter 29

Grace stood beside Alaxandar, smiled into his cold eyes, and wished there was another way. To cause the death of her own flesh and blood would forever leave her broken. Hatred of him, and disgust with what she was capable of, would always darken her life.

But now, she had a part to play. "Grandpapa, dance with me?"

She watched him survey the small crowd in the ballroom, signal one of his henchmen, and miraculously, the dance floor emptied.

Everyone watched him lead the young woman in the flowing golden dress to the center of the room. He lifted her left hand to his shoulder, took her right hand and held it in one sweaty palm, the other pressed into the small of her back.

All conversation stopped, making the music seem to grow louder. Everyone watched them.

Grace moved fluidly despite being an awkward six inches taller than her partner. She kept a faint smile on her face, and leaned down slightly to listen as he spoke to her.

"You look nothing like Katarina, but you have her grace, my dear."

"Thank you. From Isaac I inherited my height, my coloring, and my tenacity."

He smiled slyly. "And what about from your mother?"

"Meredith is responsible for my steely resolve."

He chuckled. "Did you fuck Isaac as she did?"

So shocked by the words, it took a moment for her to realize he meant them in the literal sense. She ground out coolly, "What makes you think I'm not a virgin?"

His nostrils flared ever so slightly. "With your physical attributes you'd be worth a great deal untouched." He slid his hand lower and pressed her relentlessly against him, thrusting his leg between hers so she could feel his hard-on against her thigh.

She nearly choked on the words caught in her throat, and she glared into his shiny black eyes. *Killing you will be easy. I could put a knife in your heart right here, right now…*

Grace!

Startled, she glanced around and was shocked to see Logan at the edge of the dance floor. Before she could stop them, the words, *Get me out of here* flew toward him, but they were followed by a quick command of *No! Not yet. Wait.*

A sudden commotion at the open French doors drew everyone's attention away from the dance floor. An old woman in an elegant black dress, with jewels dripping from her earlobes, was being held between two guards. But when Alaxandar spoke in rapid Russian, the music stopped, and the woman was instantly released. She shook herself, straightened her dress, and strolled slowly toward them.

"Katarina," his voice dripped sarcasm. "Must you

always make such an entrance?" He released his grip on Grace and stepped toward the woman he'd made a child with.

She smiled up at him. "Alaxandar, how nice to see you again."

"I must dance with the diva," he announced. At his nod, music once again filled the room and he held out his arms to Katarina.

Grace walked straight to Logan. *What's going on? What are you doing here? Why is my grandmother here?*

He wrapped his arms around her, began to move slowly to the music. *Just dance with me for a minute. I've missed you.*

Katarina watched Logan circle Grace toward the open doors, then turned her attention to the man she loathed.

"Well, Katarina, what brings you to my arms tonight?"

"I've come to say goodbye."

"You're leaving?"

"No, you are."

He frowned. "Don't be ridiculous, I am king. This is my home, my country, and I never leave here."

"She isn't yours. Isaac wasn't yours."

"What did you say?"

"You heard me. My son's father was a wildly romantic Argentinean polo player. You have no blood ties to my granddaughter, and I will not ever see your hands on her again."

He sneered. "And who shall stop me. You?" He looked down his nose at her. The top of her head barely reached his chin. "You're nothing but a washed up old woman." His grin became evil. "I'm going to have her tonight. Perhaps you should watch."

"You'd rape her because she's not your blood?" The disgust in her voice came nowhere close to expressing the hatred running through her veins. And what she was about to do suddenly became very, very, easy.

"I intend to have her tonight. Her blood means nothing to me. Nothing until I see it on my sheets."

Katarina tried to pull away, but he held fast. "I will kill you with my bare hands," she snarled with deadly quiet.

And from somewhere behind the orchestra there was a whisper, "You won't have to old woman." And Sergei's fingertip squeezed ever so slightly. He was out of the room before Alaxandar fell to the floor.

Katarina stood over him, frozen, staring at the red dot of blood on his forehead. When a guard ran forward and shoved her aside, she glanced over at Grace standing in the doorway with Logan's arm firmly around her shoulders.

#

Grace refused to leave with Logan, instead, she stayed behind with Katarina. They eventually traveled to Zurich together where she finally met Francesco, Isaac's biological father. Then they flew back to Argentina with him, met an entire swarm of Grace's tall, golden-eyed relatives before she returned home.

Life went on. She went on. But didn't.

She sent both Milo and Careless to live at Paradise with the girls they'd rescued from the dance school. The children spent hours experiencing the unconditional love of her pets. Everyone was happy.

Aanna had fallen head over heels for Farley, and was taking riding lessons on lesser beasts twice a day, so she'd soon be allowed to ride the big black gelding.

Caroline was happy to have Sergei home again. Sarah was blissfully in love with Dr. Kelton, and had given up her practice to work with him at ETC.

Even Katarina was moving forward, spending time in Argentina with Francesco at his famous vineyard nestled among the foothills of the Andes. They'd decided to get to know one another better than they had when their paths had crossed at a fancy party in Spain so many years before.

But Grace's recovery stalled. She'd promised Logan she'd call him when she was ready to move on, but weeks went by and she remained somewhat lost, emotionally empty and untouchable, as though a wall of glass stood between her and the rest of the world... until Katarina advised her to dance.

Each day she put on the music. Followed the steps. And allowed her mind to put the entire picture together. The pieces fell neatly into place, and there was no longer any doubt. Kelton had maneuvered her into position. She and Logan had both been manipulated. Even Kusavinski had been part of the master plan. But it didn't matter anymore. Evil had been stopped. Period.

Little by little, the door to her soul creaked open and she began to feel again.

#

Logan had waited long enough.
Nancy slipped her hand into the slot and the security

light blinked green. She glanced sideways at Logan and muttered, "I hope you know what you're doing."

"I do."

"She sleeps with a gun under her pillow, so for Christ's sake, be careful."

"Nancy..."

"Yeah, I know, you're a big bad agent, not afraid of a mere woman."

He chuckled. "She's not just any woman, and when she's not pissing me off, she scares me half to death." He shook his head. "But it's time."

He pushed open the door, leaned down and kissed Nancy on the cheek. "Thanks. Now go home."

He slipped inside, reengaged the security, and waited, letting all his senses roam, searching for her, finding her easily, in the studio.

He opened the door and his heart turned over. She was sitting cross-legged in the middle of the polished wood floor staring at the wall. He stepped inside and followed her gaze to the new panel. It was the picture of her and Isaac, dancing *Renaissance*, mere hours before their world had imploded.

"Grace."

She felt rooted to the spot, only her eyes moved while the rest of her hung in limbo, waiting, wishing, not knowing what she should do, could do. Was it too late to go back? Would her life ever be anything but chaotic emotions interspersed with real life trauma? She stared at him. The man, the agent, her friend, and lover. And wished life had been different. Wished she'd been able to make better decisions. She longed for the strength that seemed to permeate her bones when he touched her. His touch, those hands. She closed her eyes to fight back the tears beginning to well. And then, as though she had no choice, the iron door to her mind allowed two words to slip out.

Touch me.

"Look at me, Grace."

Slowly, her lids raised, the golden eyes were soft, vulnerable, her heart was right there.

"Come here." His voice was deep and sure.

She stood. Simply moved one foot after the other until she was wrapped in his arms, her face buried in his throat. She inhaled his scent and felt her body vibrate right down to her toes. She was still alive. Her skin tingled where his breath caressed her temple, her heart thumped hard and sure against his. She lifted her face, stared into his eyes and whispered, "Love me please, Logan. Love me."

A half chuckle rumbled from deep in his chest and he said, "For the love of God, Grace, I've done nothing else since the first time I laid eyes on you." His smiling mouth lowered slowly, gently teasing hers. "Drop-dead fucking gorgeous, and the most annoying woman on earth. You slipped into my mind, and became my life's mission. You nearly cost me everything, but it made no difference. I'm yours, you're mine, we're one damned heartbeat, and you're not going anywhere without me ever again."

She lifted an eyebrow. "Really?"

"Yeah, really. So get used to it."

She smiled as she pressed her body against the full length of his. "Dance with me, Brontosaurus."

The End

Dear reader,

I sincerely hope you enjoyed this story as much as I loved writing it!

As an author, I spend most of my time alone with my computer in a room I call my writing cave, and have little interaction with my readers.

Because of this, when someone loves one of my stories and takes a minute to leave a review on Amazon or one of the other sites, spontaneous happy dancing happens in the writing cave!

And not to worry, Wolfe and Bear, my obnoxious tuxedo cats are no longer offended by this silliness.

So if you'd like to make me happy, happy, happy, and imagine me jumping around the room like an idiot, just click on my book on Amazon and leave me a review. And honestly? You don't need think of it as one of those dreaded book reviews we had to do in school. A simple, "great story" or "good read" or "interesting characters" will thrill me to no end.

And if you didn't like the book? Well, kudos for reading to the end anyways, and I hope your next reading experience is happier.

Cheers!
Kathryn.

"do not tell me No"

KATHRYN JANE

Ten floors above the Vegas Strip... the bathroom door opened and my life went down the toilet.

This being a first for me, I hadn't given much thought to the morning after a one night stand. I suppose I'd expected him to leave. Huh. One more item for the "wrong again" column.

Waking up to a flushing sound was my first clue. Then the door opened and there he was.

Tall, dark, handsome and sexy as hell, wearing nothing but a pair of faded-in-all-the-right-places, thigh-hugging jeans. Fly still fastened. Top button? Not. A line of silky dark hair aimed like a laser pointer. A living cliché. Yup, all the rest was there too, the required six pack, pecs, biceps, and shoulders, all tucked into smooth golden skin. City girls would tag him "buff." Country girl like me? Speechless, barely able to breathe.

Closing my eyes won't make him less enticing because his gut clenching male scent was lodged in my nostrils. Keeping my eyes open doesn't seem to be a better option. He's right there. Six feet of body-humming, smiling male. My face flamed at the sudden slide-show of memories.

Instinct was urging me to jump out of this

playground-sized bed and run screaming from the room but I'm buck-naked and it's a classy hotel. Still, I'd be hard to catch that way. Or I could drag a six-hundred thread-count sheet from the bed and—

"Don't even think about it." While commanding, his voice was low and sexy - as it had been all night.

Do I detect a hint of laughter? Is he reading my mind?

"Maddy?"

Not my real name, but I like the way he says it—part of what got me into this embarrassing mess. My first, morning-after-a-one-night-stand. What the hell had I been thinking? Well, actually, it was curiosity about monkey sex. Note to self, cut back on steamy novels. But they'd started me wondering, pondering, wishing? Oh yeah, I know—be careful what you wish for.

"Maddy."

I gave in, opened my eyes and there he was, standing beside the bed, watching me.

Holy jumpin' Jehoshaphat. He was beyond beautiful. His mouth, surrounded by the requisite sexy stubble was perfect, sinful. He smiled and my heart made for the exit like an angry calf on the end of a rope.

Even his strong white teeth were perfect.

His eyes, a deep sensuous blue, outlined by even darker navy, were filled with humor. He was laughing at me. No doubt my hair was a tangled mess from hours of delicious romping and I likely had raccoon eyes by now.

"What?" Lord did my voice actually squeak?

"You're freakin' out, aren't you?"

Okay, nail on the head, but did he need to know for sure? Could I bluff my way through this? I'd been known to win the odd hand of poker—but never when I was naked.

He planted one knee on the bed and leaned dangerously close, bracing himself with a hand on either side of my shoulders, his face mere inches away. I could smell toothpaste. And man. Oh man. My body went on full alert. My mind switched to hibernate. He lowered his mouth, inch by painstaking inch. I was beyond help. I wanted this, him. To heck with the consequences.

But in the last hundredth of a second, somewhere in my mind, a voice screamed, "Morning Breath!" I zipped down the bed, beyond his grasp, and bolted for the bathroom as fast as my feet would carry me… and refused to think about what my bare ass looked like in retreat.

The Intrepid Women Series

Daring
to Love

KATHRYN JANE

Galen wound his way through the chaos of giant ceramic flower pots. He'd spotted Liz at the far end of the patio. With her head lolled to one side and arms hanging limp over the edge, she almost looked dead, but not quite. He imagined putting his hand on her shoulder to wake her up and having her smile up at him. Right. She'd swing first, ask questions later. In the name of self-preservation, he whispered her name and was startled to feel his words gain entrance to her unguarded mind. He fought the urge to take advantage, to simply slip in and steal the answers he needed.

She turned her head, opened her eyes, pinned him mid step with her dead-sexy, sleepy gaze. He didn't dare get closer. Not until he figured out what kind of mood she was in.

Her voice went with the look. "Sorry."

Soft and sexy crawled over his skin. Wondering which doorway led to her bedroom, he swallowed hard. This was the Liz he'd always suspected lay under the surface. Silent and still, he waited, hoped.

She sat up, back going straight and shoulders stiffening. "I was stupid mad. Should've had it out with Mike."

Well, crap. Her change of tone washed over him like cold water. "About what?"

She swung around to put her feet on the deck and shoved a hand through her hair. "He's trying to manipulate me into spilling my guts. Took Fred away, made us go overland instead of in the Piper so we'd be stuck together for longer. Gave you orders to search my mind."

He shook his head. "No orders, just a parting shot to figure out what the next move should be. I thought Fred belonged to Mike."

She rubbed her palms on her bare knees, tugged at the hem of her baggy shorts. "He's a team member. As in ETC ID and serious skills. Mike assigned him to me while I recovered from the Australia debacle. Dog's a good listener, knows when I need to lean on him."

Galen had closed the space between them while she'd talked and then made what could be a stupid move. He crouched in front of her, laid his hands over hers to still them and looked into eyes that always made him think of stormy oceans and sex. Well, probably sex was first.

"I'm a good listener, and only a little offended you prefer Fred over me. I haven't been assigned to pick at your mind."

"Then why *are* you with this team?"

He was going to lie, straight-faced and looking her square in the eye. "A combination of reasons." At least that much was true. "I happened to be in the area, we've worked well together before, and I can fly us anywhere we need to go."

She narrowed her gaze and studied his face, looking sceptical. "Well fine. Just stay out of my mind while you're busy being so helpful."

He took her chin in his hand, let his thumb play across her bottom lip and dropped his voice an octave. "Don't you think this whole situation would come together better if you'd let me in, work with me instead of pushing me away?"

He picked up just the faintest hoarseness when she answered. "Double entendre Galen? You workin' me?"

He leaned in and she didn't retreat. "Oh, you're work all right, lady." And he kissed her with deliberate slowness, savoured the taste of her. Nobody. Not one other woman had ever come close to the taste that was Liz—and Lord but he'd sampled enough of them to know.

Her hand slipped around the back of his neck, fingers slid through his hair and she groaned, "damn you," against his lips.

The heat hit him like a lightning strike. Speared straight down. He stood, pulled her with him and slid his hands to her ass. Lifted. Then froze. He dragged his mouth away, wrapped his arms around her and held on while he gathered a few brain cells, identified the voice.

Acknowledgements

I'm told it takes a village to raise a child. As my books are my children, I have a village to thank, so here goes.

Many thanks to: author L. j. Charles for your wonderful critiquing skills and advice; Barb and Donna for the sharp-eyed reading; Judi Fennell of www.formatting4U.com for the awesome copy edits, formatting, and uploading services; Kim Killion for the fabulous cover; Scarlet E. for the picture in my head when I wrote about Fred; Lincoln City, Oregon for the hospitality; Cherry Adair for her no-nonsense encouragement (virtual butt kicking); Brenè Brown for Daring Greatly—an inspiration to me and my characters; Sandy James for encouraging me to rock the words; Al for keeping me and the pets loved, fed, and cared for while I was immersed in this story; Wolfe and Bear for the purring company while I was holed up in the writing cave, and for not minding how loud I cranked the music; Barb and Judy—how do I put it into words? You have loved and supported me my entire life. You are the constants in my journey. You've egged me on and believed in me, always. I love you both.

About the Author

Award winning author Kathryn Jane writes about the kind of women she'd like to hang out with—smart, self-reliant, think on their feet ladies who are just as happy eating a loaded hot dog at a ballgame as they are sipping champagne in the back of a limo. Women who laugh as hard as they cry, appreciate good sweaty sex, and know how to keep a secret.

Kathryn lives in a cottage on the west coast of Canada with her very own prince charming. Among her favorite things are the smell of the ocean, crisp sunny days, the warm breath of a horse, cats with a sense of humor, dogs that love to please, music, and kind people. She collects beach glass and rocks, has a single string of tiny Christmas lights that she turns on all year round, and loves to walk on the beach with her sisters.

For more information about Kathryn and her other books, check out her website, or join her on facebook and twitter.

http://kathrynjane.com/
www.facebook.com/kathryn.jane.921
https://twitter.com/@Author_Kat_Jane

Other books by Kathryn Jane

Intrepid Women Book 1 - **DO NOT TELL ME NO**
    Kindle http://amzn.to/1d1hFLR
    Print http://amzn.to/1cdTycs

Intrepid Women Book 2 - **TOUCH ME**
    Kindle …. http://amzn.to/1fhFFhQ
    Print …. http://bit.ly/NpagQ1

Intrepid Women Book 3 – **DARING TO LOVE**
    Kindle ….
    http://www.amazon.com/dp/B00I13NB9U
    Print …. http://bit.ly/1d8Wq0w

Intrepid Women Book 4 – **VOICES**
    Kindle ….
    Print ….